LYNN'S ADVENTURES: BOOK 1

Alyssa L LaRosa

DORRANCE
PUBLISHING CO
EST. 1920
PITTSBURGH, PENNSYLVANIA 15238

Dorrance Publishing Co
585 Alpha Drive
Pittsburgh, PA 15238
Visit our website at *www.dorrancebookstore.com*

ISBN: 978-1-6386-7280-7
eISBN: 978-1-6386-7631-7

Names and places are made from my imagination, or from mythology books for fictional use, or from part of my name for creativity.

LYNN'S ADVENTURES: BOOK 1

Alyssa L LaRosa

Contents

Chapter 1

Wearing fancy dresses and jewelry isn't my kind of thing like most girls. To the best of my knowledge, I prefer to wear trousers and a tunic when riding a horse. My parents despised my choice of clothing until they were murdered, but sadly no one knows who had murdered them because it happened in the middle of the night. So as my right, I am the only heir to the land and a big home my parents had. Now being a noblewoman I am free to wear what I want and do what I want while also getting whatever boring paperwork done as well.

At the age of nineteen, where eighteen and older are considered adults and adults are expected to get any work given done. As for me, I still headed out to the stables where my favorite mare, Rosalina, is being kept knowing I still had some responsibilities left to do. Can a woman like me at least have a break from so much responsibility for my small village?

I wasn't gone long though because as I had come back my handmaiden was calling for me as I was going to put Rosalina back in her stall.

"Lady Lynn! You had me so worried!"

Poor Liv, a mother of three beautiful children at the age of twenty-five, she always ended up acting like a mother figure to me after she married one of my stable boys. Shaking her head, her curly bobbed hair was bouncing on her shoulders. Being only five foot six and me five foot four, she seems like a giant to me.

"I am so sorry, Liv, I couldn't help myself from taking a break from everything." I genuinely felt guilty because she more or less raised me until I was able to do most things on my own when I was eighteen.

"Lady Lynn, I forgive you, but we have guests that have come to seek your presence." Liv waits patiently for me to say or do something and I smiled at her, "Well, take me to my room and have one of our servants keep our guests occupied as I clean myself up and look more presentable for them." She nodded and we hurried as fast as we could to get me cleaned up from my short ride with my mare.

In about an hour I was finally presentable in my dark purple day gown that doesn't poof out but is snug against my body making it more modest as I wear a locket that has a portrait of my parents. I checked my braids to see if they were perfect so that I look proper. I made sure I had on the right shoes that went perfect with the purple dress I headed out of my room and into the waiting room to greet my guests.

To my surprise, it was the Astleys of the noble family. "Lord and Lady Astley, and their son Sebastian Astley, what a wonderful surprise to see all of you here in my humble home." Not being too surprised, Sebastian never paid me any attention when we met as children; to be frank, it did not bother me because he has a million girls fawning over him to this day. Yes, he is a really handsome noble with black hair, forest green eyes, and a strong build like all noble-born sons should have in order to help fight to defend their province of their small village.

"Lady Lynn, I am sure you are aware that it is the time when you need to get married," said Lord Astley.

Feeling a bit sad about it I nod. "Yes, I am aware that it is high time I find a suitor to get married." They smiled at me and gestured towards Lord Sebastian Astley. "It is why we have brought our only son Sebastian to have two strong noble blood borns like you to be married. We also have heard you are a great fighter amongst your own village so why not have two greatest warriors and nobles to defend both villages at once and nothing can stop them."

Later that day, my handmaiden Liv came in and bowed to me, "Lady Lynn, our village priest has come to seek an audience with you." "Bring him—" my words were cut off as soon as I heard children screaming and I grabbed the sword over the mantle and ran out the door and whistled for my mare. Rosalina came galloping towards me and I hopped on her back and had her gallop towards the sound of children screaming.

We stopped at the edge of the forest and I hopped off as soon as I saw the small children running out of the forest. "Children, hop on. Rosalina will take you home." I hurriedly put the small boy and girl on her and told her what she needed to do. Like a cheetah, she ran off back to the other side of the dirt road to the village. Wolf howling is a sign that their territory was breached. Walking slowly with no fear into the forest, I stood my ground as I saw the alpha wolf growling at me. I kneeled and showed my submission and spoke, "Please forgive my people for coming into your territory. The kids will be kids and for their mistakes, I will take full responsibility for their actions."

I stayed like that for a long while for what felt like hours until the growling stopped and the sound of padded paws came to me and the alpha male wolf nudged my cheek to forgive me and the little ones. I looked up and smiled and petted him behind the ears.

"I am forever thankful for your forgiveness for me and my people. When next we meet I will give you the mightiest of names."

He whined a happy sounding whine and licked my cheek then trotted back to his pack and his territory. I walked out of the forest and back to my village to hear some cheers and to see the guests that had gathered at my home there, shocked but cheering for my success. "Listen, my people of Estonia! I have saved you all from an awful fate of death. The wolves of the forest have forgiven the mistakes of the children who should have never left this village without adults to accompany them. They are giving up a lot for us; they let us use the trees of their forest to build our homes. They let us hunt some of their prey to feed our families, so do not disrespect them by exploring the forest unsupervised." They all became silent and nodded then I went to greet the Astleys and Father Larry.   "Lady Lynn, that was remarkable for what you did," commented Father Larry.

Nodding, I grabbed the reins of Rosalina and walked the path to my home with the others following me close behind.

"So Father Larry, what brought you to come to see me?" I asked him as nicely as possible.

We stopped walking to look at the priest. Not going to guess, Sebastian was already leaning against a tree nearby, bored as hell like he doesn't want to be here. "Lady Lynn, I came to tell you something the night your parents made me promise not to tell you until the time was right, so now is the time." I nodded to encourage him to go on because I needed to know what it was they made the priest keep something important from me. "The night your brave parents were murdered they knew they had to hide the real origin of who you are. Legend has it once a girl comes of age to tame most fearsome predators in the woods, meaning the wolves, she would become the true Queen of Estonia." I looked at Father Larry confused and signaled him to elaborate.

"Lady Lynn, they were murdered because the murderers thought your parents were true rulers of Estonia. They spoke to me hours before they were murdered."

I stood there frozen in shock at the news of why my parents were murdered. Feeling all eyes on me, voice shaky as I finally spoke, "So they and you still have no clue who murdered them?" Father Larry nodded solemnly.

"Father Larry, thank you so much for telling me this after three years of complete darkness." I walked alone as all eyes followed me from close behind.

Now I know what I need to do. I need to find more answers to my questions. Who murdered my parents? Who sent them after them when it should have been me who should have died? Why am I part of the legend that has be-come the true queen of my village?

"Father Larry, since you are higher than my status it is up to you to announce this to the people of Estonia." I put Rosalina in her stall and let my number one stable boy that is married to my handmaiden take care of her as I headed to my bedchamber to clean up and think about everything that was said and done to me today. So much has happened, I need time to think. First being suited for Lord Sebastian then to saving the Estonian children and then to finally learning a bit more behind my parents' deaths. "I will find the person who leads the deaths of my parents and that person will regret messing with the LaRosa family."

Chapter 2

Late that night we all were in bed until I heard some shushing sounds and I grabbed my family sword then headed quietly down the stairs to see unwanted visitors. All dressed in black with faces covered in black masks so I and no one could identify them.

"So, you came back here to finish off the last member of LaRosa's, huh?" Silence and the tallest one seemed fast and came barreling at me, and with quick reflexes I dodged and grabbed the family sword from the mantle and deflected the attack for my side from the stranger's short sword. Now his friend tried to come at me until I saw Sebastian fighting him off for me with an elegant sword I had never seen before. When he and the short attacker came into the light, I noticed that Lord Sebastian's features were different from before.

Sebastian is an elf?! Then does that make his parents an Elf too? Distracted for a moment, the tall stranger I was fighting took my distraction to his advantage and left a scratch on my thigh. Luckily I was quick to recover and dodged the fatal attack he planned on landing on me. Kicking his feet from underneath him, I took that moment to thrust my family sword into his abdomen. Now remembering Sebastian I looked over to him and got prepared to help him to see that he and what seemed like to me his parents who now changed into elves had already finished up with their fight and were waiting for me.

"Well after we get rid of these bodies I will need answers to who you three Astley's are," I said as if I was not surprised, but to be completely honest nothing really surprises me anymore if I am discovering new things that don't seem normal.

It took all four of us about half an hour to get rid of the bodies and half of my servants to help get rid of evidence that there was a fight here. "Lord and Lady Astley, can either of you explain to me why you three are elves after centuries of not catching sight of any of you?" Sebastian and his not caring act are the same but Lady Astley says, "We are not truly Sebastian's parents, but rather he is the king of Lorali. As for who we are, Princess Lynn of Estonia, I am Aria Lotus of the Lotus family. My companion is Argos Draco of the Draco family." I look at Sebastian to see if he will tell me anything else.

"I am King Sebastian Knight. My family has been long gone since you came into existence so if you wonder how old I am it is best to know that I am older than I look."

Nodding, I take this moment of silence to think of what else needs to be done. "What are the reasons for a king and his two loyal guards to be here in my future kingdom?"

"Princess Lynn, we actually did come here for the known timing of you being married, but we also came because we knew around this time you would be in danger and would need to be protected from the dangers worse than the dangers we faced tonight," Lady Aria said with honesty.

I waited for more information on how they knew all this, but one thing is for sure, elves are the oldest beings here than the average human like me. Hearing what Lady Aria told me; that I need to leave my own home in Estonia to go somewhere safe till all of us solve how to get rid of this danger she spoke of. Finally making a decision knowing my people are in danger if I stayed here weak and unable to defend them from this powerful being who is yet to show its ugly face.

"I will come with you three, but the problem is, how will my people take it when I just up and leave?" Lady Aria and Lord Argos smiling, they changed into me and King Sebastian. "So I am guessing certain elves can shapeshift into anything?" The decoy me nods.

"Well, I shall have my handmaid Liv pack my things I need and have her husband my head stable boy Jack saddle my mare and King Sebastian's stallion for the journey to Lorali." I left all three of them discussing further plans while I walked tiredly to the west wing where my room is located to get changed into a tunic and trousers for travel and check on the family blade that was covered in blood to see if it's cleaned enough to carry on my way to Lorali.

Later on in the night, I was ready to go in a tunic and trousers and I am situated next to my mare Rosalina with my small pack of clothes and my family sword strapped to her saddle. Petting her I spoke in a soft tone so she knows how much I care for her and how I trust her to carry me through this long journey to Lorali, "Rose my sweet mare, I trust you can carry me as far as you can go as you follow King Sebastian's stallion Thunder." I was lucky enough to read the nametag on the stallion's bridle so if anything spooks them I am able to calm them down.

"Ready, Princess?" King Sebastian said with a smirk.

"Well, of course, King Sebastian, I always know when I am ready. Are you ready, King?" I responded sarcastically.

His smirk faded as I struck a nerve and we mounted our horses and trotted off. This adventure is the beginning and I hope it will end eventually so I can return to my home I have grown up in and know. For now, I must stay safe and find answers on who ordered the deaths of my parents and who is wanting me dead. I will not stop until this evil force is gone from this plane of existence and everyone is living in peace and harmony with each other no matter the race. *I will die trying to bring peace to my home and to many homes in the future. My sacrifices will be told by bards for centuries to come.*

In the forest where I met the alpha wolf, King Sebastian led us on a long journey to the kingdom of Lorali. "King Sebastian, I will need to be trained for the future battles to come because we both know this is not gonna end so quickly until the evil behind the scenes has been vanquished." He only nodded and we rode in silence.

Chapter 3

By nightfall, we stopped in a clearing a few miles from my Kingdom of Estonia. "I will hunt for us to eat tonight over the fire," said King Sebastian with a tone of not caring about the present events that happened today. Unable to speak out of hunger and tiredness, I only nodded as a response. He left as I started the fire and sat near Rosalina to calm her as well as myself from the future place I will be staying in. *I had to be engaged to the King of Lorali. Out of all the other women out there they chose me because of a prophecy. That, in all honesty, doesn't sound fair to the others who had set their eyes on him. Ugh! Why me?*

King Sebastian came back with some rabbits and cooked them over the fire. It did not take but a mere few minutes to cook the meat over the fire. We both ate in silence till we heard some rustling noise and we both drew swords ready to fight if we needed to. A few seconds later the alpha wolf I met yesterday came with an elf. "King Sebastian, I have come to tell you that there are great conflicts amongst our people."

The elf with silver hair and green slanted eyes bowed as King Sebastian spoke, "I truly am thankful, Fenri, for your message. You may hurry on back to Lorali to see if you can help not make bloodshed appear. Princess Lynn and I will be there by tomorrow evening." The silver-haired elf left in a hurry and the wolf stayed behind and I smiled. "Well met, alpha." The alpha wolf nodded. "I shall name you Hermes after the messenger god." The alpha wags his tail and nuzzles my hand and I pet him.

"So once we get to the Kingdom of Lorali is there anything I can do to help with the conflicts?"

He jerked his head to me and I was confused at his sudden reaction and asked him, "What is wrong?" With wide eyes clearly showing how shocked he was, he said, "Me and my advisor were speaking our native tongue. We were speaking Elvish and you somehow knew what our conversation was." In complete shock, I seemed to remember how it is true that elves don't speak English around humans due to distrust, but I truly think it's part of the prophecy. "King Sebastian, do you think me being able to understand your language is part of the prophecy?"

He scratched the back of his neck to think, then replied calmly, " I am unsure. When we get there I will have some of my people do research on this and report to me about it because I truly am stumped for the first time in a hundred years."

I was still shocked and I can't explain it myself no matter how hard I try to think of excuses on how I can understand them, but one thing I do know is I can't speak their language. Maybe, who knows.

Chapter 4

Later this evening we arrived at Lorali, and one of his elven handmaidens took me to where I was going to stay and helped get me cleaned up from the journey. I already knew that Hermes left as soon as we got to the entrance to the Kingdom of Lorali. King Sebastian and I went our separate ways and did separate things. For example, King Sebastian had his trusted advisor from before named Fenri show me around Lorali while also giving me tips to shortcuts to get to certain places, which helped a lot. Then we came up to the archery range, and I became excited because I loved archery more than swordplay. I instantly took a bow with some arrows near the others and stood about a hundred feet from the target and took aim and released my first arrow.

I heard gasps of shock and awe and in their language. I heard them whisper that I made a bulls-eye from my first shot and we all knew I am human and no mere human like me is capable of getting a bullseye in one go. I am human I admit but I am also from a prophecy to become Queen of Estonia. I try to see if I missed this time, but again I hit the same bulls-eye.

"Hmmm... Lord Fenri, I believe I am going to not

have much fun with this range if I make a bulls-eye ten times in a row." Fenri nodded in agreement and said in my tongue, "Perhaps if you duel with one of our soldiers maybe they can help be a fitting challenge for you Princess Lynn."

I nodded in excitement, and Lord Fenri led me to the dueling field where soldiers practice their swordplay with each other, and I drew my sword waiting for an elf soldier to come and duel me. A few minutes later, a tall blond elf soldier with green eyes and a slim, elegant build came forward saying nothing and we took our stances together.

I have no clue how long we both stood there waiting for the other to make the first move. Then, in a quick motion, he was coming at me, and I parried his first attack aimed at my knees. We fought and parried, but he seemed to not be breaking a sweat, but as for me I was about to fall to the ground exhausted. I can not match an ancient being's stamina because they are naturally slim and built for these kinds of things.

Before I could focus on what was happening, I was on the ground panting and looking up the blade of a slim-looking sword and at my opponent the blond elf. I smiled, panting from exhaustion. "That was a great fight, young blond elf. I am truly thankful for the challenge you and your people have given me." He nodded and stood up and walked off then we all heard an angry King Sebastian and I flinched. *Shit! Here comes the king. Hopefully he doesn't get upset at Lord Fenri for showing me a challenging fight to occupy my time.*

"Why is Princess Lynn in this practice field when

she needs to be in my castle cleaning herself up and resting?" His tone was menacing and stern so I decided to defend everyone. "King Sebastian, it was me who wanted to be here on the days I have nothing more to do, especially if it helps train me against the enemy of my family."

He huffed and turned back in the direction where his beautiful palace stands and Lord Fenri and I followed him close behind. Soon we were all inside, and King Sebastian dismissed Lord Fenri and I was actually relieved he wasn't in trouble, but now it is only me and the king in the massive hallway of his palace. Without notice I was pinned against a wall with his hands on both sides of my head and I blushed and my heart skipped a beat and all I thought out of the blue was being kissed by him. "A princess who is soon to be queen after all this should have freshened up and gotten some rest instead of tiring herself more with man's work." He sounded concerned for me and I felt happy and excited all at once, but I tried my best to quell the thoughts that were about sex and the kiss because right here and now was not the time to act like a spoiled rich girl.

I nodded and said, "I truly understand your concerns, King Sebastian, but it was my choice to train a little more before I came here."

He lifted my chin with his finger and his thumb brushing my bottom lip and the light touch he is giving me now is making me feel the ache of him kissing me and touching me more. My heart is racing and my face flushes. I waited for his next move until a different advisor came to interrupt us and we jumped and he was like his old self when we met. The advisor whispered in his ear, and he eventually nodded the advisor's dismissal and he faced me again with concern written all over his face. "Please, Lynn, go get cleaned up to then get some rest if possible and meet me at the dining hall. My hand-maids will take turns seeing to you so you can feel welcome here." He walked off, and I stood there in the midst of confusion of what just happened until one of his maids came to collect me to the room where I would be staying till the war is over.

I awoke to the sound of knocking and my name. I groaned from how stiff my body felt after the long travels and the excess of the duel I had with one of the soldiers here in Lorali. Looking out the window, I realized it is night time and I am needed to get ready for the evening meal and listen to the stuff I am needed to do in order to return to my future kingdom, my home Estonia.

A young black-haired maid helped me get into an evening dress and look completely presentable for guests and for King Sebastian. The young maid led me to the dinning hall and showed me where I was to sit, and it was near the head of the table where the king is supposed to sit. *Well as the betrothed to the King I suppose it is only right I have to sit here.*

Few minutes later King Sebastian came in and froze at the entrance to the dining hall, and I was confused but I thought I saw a hint of a blush or I might have imagined it because as soon as it came it was gone. He acted like nothing happened, but something is up and I will find out later in his chambers alone so no one can suspect weakness in him.

We ate in silence until he finally spoke through the awkward silence, "Lynn, you look beautiful." I blushed and nodded my thanks as I spoke, "Well thank you, King Sebastian. You look dashing as well." I looked up to see a faint smirk of amusement and I ended up smiling as well.

After our meal we parted ways to our rooms, but I waited for him to be in his after I dismissed his maid to get dressed into my nightgown. A few minutes later I rushed across the hall to his bedchamber and knocked. "Come in," his voice sounded tired so I came in. "Anything you needed, Fenri?" Laughing, I said, "Well, King Sebastian, you look nice with no tunic but I had a question about what I am supposed to do to help increase my chances to return home?"

He quickly turned around and dragged me inside his room and shut the door. "You should be more lady-like in knowing what it means to be in a man's bedchamber."

I shrugged and repeated my question, "King Sebastian, what am I to do to increase my chances to go home?" His mouth was in a hard line, a sign that shows me he is in debate on telling me what he is hiding from me or not.

He sighed and turned his back to me as he spoke in a solemn tone, "Lynn, the person who had your parents murdered and later sent out to have you killed as well was my long lost enemy who I thought I had defeated. Alas I have learned he has changed his looks and his name and is ruling a kingdom four days from here called Mara."

He grabbed me in his arms and held me tight and it was a surprise. "I don't want you to get hurt or killed by my ancient enemy who I should have defeated." I hear the worry and sadness in his voice, and I can also feel it in his embrace so I hugged him back. "Sebastian, it is okay. I believe I am destined to help you defeat him once and for all." Out of the blue I felt his lips against mine and his hand knotting in my hair and I kissed him back. I never knew how strong this feeling was for him. As we kissed I wanted him more, but he pulled apart and we both ended up panting for air.

"We can't do that here and now because it is not the right time."

I felt a pang of guilt and embarrassment for wanting more than the fevered kiss that passed between us, but deep down I also knew that now is not the time to have sex after everything that is happening. "I understand, Sebastian, so can you tell me more about this long ancient enemy of yours?" He nods. " You may need to sit or lay on the bed because it will be a long story of how I met the ancient King named Asmodeus who is now known to you as Wolfson." I laid on the bed instead of sitting knowing after his story I would end up asleep.

Chapter 5

"A long, long time ago, when I was your age, nineteen, and way before you were ever born, my friend Asmodeus who is known today as King Wolfson was actually a great man till a few weeks later, something completely changed and it changed him into someone I don't know.

"He was not the elf of kindness and care; he became the Onno, or in your language a demon. My father King Erin and mother Queen Isa exiled my friend, but my friend looked at me with a fake look of begging me to help him stay. I knew if I helped him stay, he wouldn't be the same friend I once knew before and wouldn't return so I had my back turned to him as a sign I couldn't help someone who murdered innocent animals that were a part of our people's essence.

"After a few weeks he came back and assassinated my parents, and when I turned twenty-five I was named king of Lorali and left to fight Asmodeus with a handful of really skilled fighters, but most of them never truly survived the fight against him. As for me, I was successful in defeating him, or so I thought.

"It has been a hundred years since then, and to find out your own parents were murdered gave me the idea it was Asmodeus who is now called King Wolfson. I have discovered how he survived the battle a hundred years ago. He used an ally that looks so much like him to sub in for him so I killed the ally and not him."

He looks sad but at the same time like a weight has been lifted and as part of my destiny I will help this man to succeed in defeating his old friend who has been his enemy for a hundred years.

"Sebastian, I promise to help you succeed in this final battle, but you and those who knew him must take turns in training me into knowing his weakness because everyone has one and we all know somewhere deep down he has one as well."

He nods and starts another story to help bring us out of the dark. "Before the battles against Asmodeus, everything was peaceful and safe.

"I was just a small, energetic elf knowing the responsibilities I would have one day when I get older. I was also a mischievous kid as well, pranking my caretakers and my guards just to spend some time with my friends.

"We all sparred with wooden swords since in the morning to the late afternoon and till my friend's parents called for them to return to their homes and I ran back home to get ready to be scolded for abandoning my guards to spend time with my friends, and one of them was Asmodeus.

"I never regretted being with them but I do regret knowing whatever happened to my old friend Asmodeus before he became King Wolfson."

I yawned finally knowing the background history of all this before I was told it was my destiny to rule Estonia and help my future husband defeat his old, long enemy, King Wolfson. I saw him smile and help tuck me into his bed and kiss my forehead, "Rest well, my beloved Lynn." Unable to comprehend what he said, I fell asleep before I could ask him what he said.

Chapter 6

I awoke to the sight of him sleeping soundly and peacefully next to me. Smiling, I gave him a light kiss and got up and headed back to my room to get dressed and head to the sparring field to duel with whoever was there today that was willing to help train me in stamina, speed, and strength.

It wasn't long till the field was full of elven soldiers sparring for the next battle. Deciding to wait, I explored the town for a bit till I headed back to my room to change into riding clothes for my horse Rosalina who I seemed to miss a lot now since I left my home to train here and plan on how to save everyone and get King Sebatian's revenge for what his ex-friend Asmodeus has caused.

I was with Rosalina for about an hour by the river and I heard human children screaming out of fear. I quickly grabbed my sword and left my sweet mare on the river bank to graze and ran to the sound of the children screaming. I soon found that we were close to a town a few miles away called Starla. The town was in flames and I soon began to hear the townspeople screaming and I risked my own life to save them and knowing I may get in trouble, but their minds will be wiped of knowledge that the elves ever existed. I told men and women who have children in their hands to hide in the woods behind me and keep going till they find a river and across it and my horse and I would meet them soon.

"Someone help! Please help my children; they've gotten stuck in our home!" I ran to the mother's side and told her I would meet her on my horse with her kids. She hesitated for a bit then ran to where the others were hidden and I ran in. Smoke made it hard to breathe and see so I only kept coughing to help clear my throat. "Kids! I am here to help you! Your mother ran to the forest for safety so hurry, tell me where you guys are so I can grab you before this place turns to rubble!"

I was walking and trying to keep my balance while listening above the sound of roaring flames that were burning the hairs off my arms, and then I heard sounds of coughing nearby and ran to them grabbed both in my arms and used my cloak to cover their little heads and ran outside to the forest.

"Kids, you are safe where we are going with your mother and the others are safe for everyone. Just don't speak till you have enough fresh air in your lungs."

A few minutes later, the mother of the kids I held rushed and took them from me. "Thank you so much young, Lady." Smiling I spoke to everyone as I got onto my horse Rosalina, "Everyone please follow me to a place that has been hidden for centuries, but when we get there you all must show respect to the place like it is your own home and to never leave till the war that has never ended before many of us were ever born."

I led Rosalina and the others in the direction to Lorali. It took us only a few hours to reach there, and I called out for the King of the elves to let him know who I had saved and brought here in his home. I hopped off and told the frightened and curious townspeople to stay close to my horse while I spoke to King Sebastian.

"What is going on here, Lynn? Why is there a whole town of humans here?" He spoke with tension and caution. I don't blame him so I told him what happened earlier when I was out riding with Rosalina and to the point of bringing them here safe since it's the closest place for them but also hidden to the world.

He was shocked and told one of his trusted advisors to help the people get settled here with new items to help make them feel at home. He turned to me as one of his soldiers took my mare to be stabled and was worried as I was covered in soot and possible burns. "Lynn, go to my bedchamber immediately so I can send in my healers to heal those burns after your bath. Then after that I expect you to be there in my room when I have finished with the duties that have kept me from you all day." He turned on his heels and left back to his palace to do more kingly duties.

After my bath, a female healer with blond hair and violet eyes who seemed to be way more beautiful than I could ever be came to check on my burns and spoke in a language a bit older than the language I heard since I arrived here yesterday. A few minutes later, she told me in my native tongue to just rest so the magic of healing could settle in and last a bit longer, and I did as I was told as I ended up trying to plan ways to be similar to the elves and how they fight to win this centuries old war and to go back home.

I was still in deep thought when I heard King Sebastian's footsteps come into the room and he took a bath. I sighed and voiced my thoughts out loud, "How can I be a bit more like you guys?"

"What do you mean?" He heard me and sounded worried but also caring as well.

"I mean, how do I last longer in a fight with better agility and with a strength to lift a trunk of a fallen oak tree?"

He soon came out completely naked, and I flushed with embarrassment and covered my eyes to not let him feel ashamed for showing me his naked, flawless skin in front of me. Then, he was uncovering my hands and was kissing me desperately, and I felt the urge to kiss him more and have more as well. We were panting as he took my nightgown off and threw it to the floor, and I realized I was completely naked.

"I-I'm embarrassed about how I am not as beautiful as the elf women here in Lorali."

I was blushing so red that he was grinning and kissing me. "Lynn, you are just as beautiful as the elf women here. In fact, you're like a goddess who needs to be worshipped." That helped me relax and feel better because I was giggling.

"You think so, King Sebastian?"

"I know so, and call me only Sebastian," he says as he grins and kisses me.

He kissed my neck, and my heart sped up and I was panting more as I moaned softly. His kisses trailed down to my chest, to my mid section then down there, and that made me gasp in pleasure. I felt his smirk, and that made me blush and pant more in excitement. He came back up to kiss me and asked, "You ready for me?" I was red as a tomato, and I nodded but was also remembering what he said yesterday.

"I thought you wanted to wait for after the war was over?"

He smirked and shrugged. "I thought so too, but after I saw you covered in soot and burns from saving the townspeople it made me think we may never live to have this moment ever again if we won this war or not." He actually made a point so I kissed him deeply and whispered in embarrassment because it was my first time. "Be gentle with me because this is my first time."

"I will, love. I promise to be gentle with you."

I felt the tip slowly slide into me, and I held my breath from the pain and I knew the new feeling made me bleed a bit because hell, it is my first time. "You feeling okay? Did I hurt you?" he asked me out of concern, and I love him for that so I shook my head no.

"No, just go slowly and it will be perfect."

He nodded and went slowly, and I could feel the pleasure coursing through my body. I began to moan as he started to pick up speed, and I bit my lip to not be too loud for his servants to hear.

Next morning I woke up naked in his bed and he was gone, probably back to his kingly duties. I got up to see my handmaid waiting for me and I headed to the powder room to clean up from the amazing adventure I had from Sebastian.

A few minutes later I came out fresh and smelling

like roses. I put on a tunic and trousers to go train in. As I was walking to the training fields Hermes was sitting at the entrance to the castle and I smiled. "Hey, Hermes, long time no see." He whines and wags his tail in excitement to see me again, and I pet him giggling like a little girl.

"Cute, I wished I met you when I was a little girl."

I spent the whole hour playing with Hermes as the elves of all ages watched me in awe. I paid them no mind because I felt the stresses of not being back home dissipate off my shoulders.

Later on I heard Sebastian's footsteps, and I smiled as I pet the sleeping Hermes's head on my lap. "Hello, Your Majesty. What can I do for you?"

"Perceptive are you, Princess?" I hear a hint of a smile in his voice and a sense of pride.

"Well I have to be in order to survive in this world right?" I look up at him and smile.

Soon a messenger came and whispered in his ear, and he frowned and said unhappily, "Already? He has made his move? Well go gather the soldiers." With a nod he left in a hurry.

"Well, when are we leaving?" I got up feeling excited to finally get out and fight.

"Oh, you are not joining us; it will be me and the trained soldiers of Lorali."

I frowned and crossed my arms giving him a look that says he won't get to have sex with me if I don't come to fight along after all the training I had. He sighed and I smiled in victory. "Fine, you can come along. We set out immediately when our men and trained women have packed and saddled their horses, and I assume you already had Rosalina saddled with everything you will need on this long journey?" I nodded and whistled for her and checked my family sword and a bought bow with the quiver of arrows then I climbed onto her back in my trousers and tunic. "Well, you wanna ride with me or ride your black stallion Thunder?"

"I will ride Thunder because Rosalina can't travel for long with both of us on her back so my advisor Fenri already had him saddled with everything I needed."

Once the army of Lorali was ready, Sebastian and I led the way to the battle field that is a few days away, long enough to plan on if his old friend will be in the battle or hiding behind his stone walls.

Smiling, I said, "Let the journey for the fight of freedom begin."

Chapter 7

.

It was soon dusk, and we set up camp for the night since we have a long way to go before we reach the plains of Tamar. I stayed in the tent made for King Sebastian but I couldn't eat or sleep due to constant thoughts of what I would do if Asmodeus was at Tamar. Groaning in frustration, I left the tent to be with my mare Rosalina.

"Hey, sweet girl. I will be with you till my train of thoughts have been quelled."

I pet her and scratched her favorite spots as I kept thinking. As if she knew what I was thinking, she nudged my side and I giggled. "Thank you for the distracting nudge. I am so glad I have you in my life, Rosalina." I smiled broadly at her brown eyes and she made a nodding motion with her head.

"Lynn, you feeling okay?" Without looking I knew who spoke to me.

"I am just thinking of your story of your friend Asmodeus and how he will end up at Tamar or not to help finish me or you off."

I finally looked up at him and I saw some sadness in his eyes and he grabbed me behind Rosalina to hug me tightly. "I hope he won't come to the battlefield of Tamar because I never want to see you get hurt or worse, dead. I love you, Lynn."

His confession shocked me and made my heart skip a beat. "Oh, Sebastian, I love you too." I smiled and kissed him then dragged him back to our tent to sleep till first light.

Light shined through our tent and all of us were up and packing up our camp. Dousing out the campfire with the dirt was boring, but it is the only way to not set the world on fire. I then checked on my mare to see that the straps for the saddle had come loose, and I rolled my eyes and tightened her saddle again then in one swift move I was in the saddle waiting for Sebastian to lead the way again where our horses trot beside each other.

"I will show your soldiers how I fight and when I should not be messed with. Especially when my horse is involved."

"I am sure you will and no doubt end up making them look weak compared to you."

He chuckles at me, and now it makes me want to show the kingdom of Lorali how strong I am as a human not because I am what the prophecy has foretold. I am stronger than I look and way smarter than most women in the world in my own opinion.

Finally we are at the battlefield where there will be lives lost due to this ancient fiend pretending to be a human king. It is night so we all set up our camps away from the field but not too terribly far just like our foes have. I was set to take the first watch while also looking far off at the enemy camp to see if I can spot the King Asmodeus from here waiting to destroy us or more or less finish off what he has started a long time ago. *"Hmmm.... What could the king be planning by just sending the men out to do his dirty work? Is this a test to see who is here and to test our strength against his army?"*

Frustrated at not being able to get the right answer on the spot, I growled at myself. "Lynn, you okay?" I turn to Sebastian and stare into his dark green eyes debating on lying, but against my better judgment I shake my head. "No, I am not, Sebastian. I have been trying to figure out if Asmodeus would be here himself just to end the fight you and him had a very long time ago."

I watched Sebastian stroke his flawless chin in thought. "I can see why you would think that, but Asmodeus is smart; he will make us use up all of our resources before we reach him so he can use that opportunity to kill us all. And to end you so the next leader of the prophecy won't try to kill him." I nod at his thinking and finally understand Asmodeus will go so far as to tire us all out to make us weak enough for him to kill.

"Thank you, and he won't tire us out because we all have trained for this and to be honest, I won't be able to keep up with you all for this but I will do my best to help make our enemies run in fear of us."

He chuckled at me, and I felt embarrassed for having such determination. Before I got to say how I felt about him chuckling at my honest words, he took my hand and dragged me to our tent as the second watch took my place. Feeling brave and determined that this battle would be the first of many we would win, I fell deep asleep.

On my mare and ready to fight without armor while soldiers of Lorali are in armor, I rode in front of Sebastian and the others to help encourage them that we would succeed.

"Ok! Listen up! This is the first battle that some of us have been in and we all may feel like we might fail! Ha! I am human, and I believe in all of us that this first of many battles we will win! Your king and I have learned that the king of our enemies is not there so we are lucky!"

I stopped to look at them all with shocked and awed faces at me, a mere human giving them the speech their king should be giving them instead.

"So let me hear your proud battle cries to the soldiers who run home to their mothers like a baby! I wanna hear you all are here because you know what you are fighting for!"

I raised my family sword, and the soldiers and Sebastian followed suit giving me a loud roar of their battle cry. I looked at Sebastian nodding that we are ready to go into battle to die trying to win this battle. He nodded back and rode first then I behind him with soldiers on foot. I cut down a man from the saddle, and it's a sign the battle has begun. And no one will escape this unharmed or alive.

Chapter 8

I was panting and covered in blood. Not quite sure whose blood, but this battle won't end till one side has less soldiers and has run away to regroup or surrender. I sliced into another enemy soldier who tried to stab my mare. He fell without understanding what happened till it was too late.

I was feeling so exhausted compared to the others on the battlefield, but I knew that I must not stop because they will take that chance to strike me down. I rode my mare to the woods and tied her there to the tree far away from battle and ran back into the fray prepared to die on the battlefield like everyone else.

As soon as I got there, most of our enemy soldiers had decreased in number so I let Sebastian and the others take care of any that threw down their weapons to take as prisoners or not as I walked around the field for any men who have survived this battle to kill or to save.

"Lynn!"

Before I could turn around to see why my name was called I was stabbed in the side. I was lucky I could dodge the fatal attack the soldier tried to lay into me. I thrust my family sword into his chest and sat on the ground. Sebastian came to my side also covered in blood not sure whose and my thoughts too hazy to even try to think about it.

"Sebastian, I am only losing blood. The wound isn't completely fatal so find your healers to help heal those of ours who survived while they tend to me last."

I can already know he was going to be upset that my wounds would be tended to last. So before I could hear his words of protest, everything went black.

I woke up to darkness outside, and I saw Sebastian pacing next to the bed and I ended up laughing. "The more you frown and worry you may end up with wrinkles even though you elves are flawless." I hear him sigh a relief as he quickly kneeled next to me and took my hand in his.

"Not funny Lynn. I was worried that you would never wake up because I forced my healers to heal the badly wounded like you said then to heal you last. It has been two days since the battle."

I looked at him wide-eyed and shocked. "Two days! Sebastian, you could have been making us travel back home to Lorali to get the soldiers healed better and faster while we regroup!" I say angrily at him. The only reaction I got from him was laughter.

"What! I am serious. We need to heal the soldiers on the homefront and to plan our next move and to figure out where the king will send his army to next."

"You never stopped being selfless. I can't wait to marry you after this war with Asmodeus." He kisses my forehead.

I ended up silent after that, but I needed to move and get up from this hard bed to see how many of us still stand and to help with the damages if need be. Trotting of hooves was coming closer to me in the dark and the dim light showed Rosalina, and I smile at my mare.

"Hey, girl. Missed me?" I pet her soft velvet nose and she nudges my hand asking how I am.

"Sweet girl, I am always fine and always will end up being the last one standing."

"Lynn, she has been fighting me and my men to get to you. I have never seen a horse act like this to their own master," Sebastian said.

I smiled at her and felt proud of her loyalty. To feel more presentable I run my fingers through my long brown hair to eradicate the tangles and flatten it against my back. As soon as I was in the middle of the camp, all the men and women who fought with me and their king cheered and breathed a sigh of relief that I was alive and I blushed from embarrassment at the attention they seem to give me and I hid my face behind Sebastian's shoulder.

I felt him smile, and I hid behind him more as a few men catcall towards me and call me cute. I felt and saw Sebastian's muscles in his whole body stiff-en, and the men stopped and apologized like they knew they offended the King because I am his fiance. Sebastian gave 'this isn't over' speech to his army as I only listened to the important key parts of our next mission to reach our goal.

We all started to pack up our war camp, but as I looked around it was only the injured and me and the King packing up to go home. *I may have missed the important part that the uninjured soldiers would stay here till we are sure that the enemy won't come back to the same place to attack us again. Crap, I may need to practice to listen to everything someone says no matter who it is and how unimportant some parts may be. Every detail is important to understand the success.*

I hopped onto Rosalina wincing from soreness in my recently healed abdomen and waited for Sebastian to lead the way back home to plan our next attack or our next defense. He rode up next to me and gave me a soft kiss then he trotted off and I next to him with the injured soldiers trailing us from behind.

Night came, and we made camp for those of us who were still injured and needed some time to heal still. I expected it for the soldiers but I am sure it was for me since I haven't completely healed yet, just stitched up. I sighed after realizing the army could go all the way home even through the night to Lorali without complaining about the wounds they suffered in battle. I would too, but I am human and most humans won't keep up the same stamina even if wounded like the elves. I feel ashamed being human but also not since I have proven to be of a huge asset to them besides being some new queen from the prophecy.

I was standing next to my mare thinking of what I should do next when we get back to Lorali until strong arms and a slender body held me from behind. "I won't train for your sake in this condition, Sebastian, but I will try to help around the kingdom and the castle in order to keep myself moving and not working so hard." I hear him laugh. "I never expected you to train but I am wondering the same as you what all of us should do once we are back home." I hear him pause for deep thought then I felt him tug at my waist to come to bed and I debated on coming with him. In order for me to heal and get better I must get as much sleep as I can in order to fight for the next battle.

We set out again, and it is my first time noticing this path looks like it will be faster to home than the last one. I should try to take notes on where I need to go in order to get back here and maybe back to Estonia one day. Not seeing a map for so long and already missing my own home, I ask for a map to borrow to look for my old home again and without question a female soldier lent me her map. I must assume she has to be a newly recruited elf if she needed a map. I unrolled the map in my saddle and looked at the locations of the kingdoms. Lorali lands in the center of the forest. Estonia lays to the right outside it on the edge of the forest. And Asmodeus, of course he would be by the sea. *Shit! Of course his castle would be by the sea. He will have an armada to control and to send out to conquer any other lands! I should have known the King would be there! We need to come up with plans for this armada in case we have to fight on the sea where the ocean will be our graves.*

We made it back to Lorali by noon and I hopped off my mare to go to Sebastian and have a talk and plan in the war room. He already sensed I wouldn't take a no for an answer so he said, "We will all get cleaned up for this meeting to discuss our next move. So once you are cleaned up have Fenri lead you to our war room." At that we rushed inside and got ready for the meeting. As I was bathing and untangling my hair with help from another female servant whose name is Helga, which I heard from others, I was thinking of many ways to help keep us all alive in case our next battle would be out on the sea. About an hour later, I am bathed and dressed in female pants and a tunic to help discuss our future.

Fenri led me to the room where I am supposed to be and I get to see a trace of worry in his face. "King Sebastian, I have seen where the enemy King has his court and it doesn't suit well for us." He raised a brow at me in question that other soldiers of high command also are curious about. "Asmodeus is by the sea which can lead to a possibility that we may have to fight him or the next army there. I must assume Lorali doesn't have an armada of our own?" Eyes widened around me and the commanders looked at Sebastian waiting for his response.

"Lynn, you are correct; we do not have an armada of our own, but we have elves like us who do and we call them the sea elves. They only live in the sea. They come to shore only to trade with us so we can get any wares they have and they can get any we have."

Nodding at this, I knew there was no other way to say it but I did, "King Sebastian, you may be mad at me for saying this, but I must. I will go to the location the sea elves are at and talk to their leader about being prepared to take most of us on board to fight on the sea." He gave me a look that could kill, but he rubbed his face with both hands in frustration and conceded.

"Fine, but I will have some soldiers here go with you by first light while the commanders and I discuss other future plans here on land. But be safe. I can't lose you,

Lynn, future Queen of Estonia and Lorali."

I blushed at those heartfelt words and bowed then had Fenri lead me back to my rooms to get changed and prepared for bed then asked Fenri to make sure my mare was ready for me by first light and to wake me when it was time to go. He bowed and promised to hold to my wishes.

Chapter 9

I layed there unable to sleep. My brain going a million miles per hour unable to slow it down to get some sleep but then, I remembered a song my mother and father used to sing to me when I was a kid unable to sleep. I quietly sung myself to sleep so I could be rested enough to ride to the docks to find the sea elves.

I was already up when Fenri came to fetch me. I smiled and I followed him to the stables to greet my mare then the rest of the soldiers. I was the first to hop onto my mare and soon the others followed suit. One of the soldiers was a commander. We followed him to the docks that belonged to the elves and the forest trail to them was a beautiful sight. If I must be honest, it is a better view than the ones I witnessed for a few weeks now.

We rode long and hard not willing to waste time in this possibility. But I felt something wrong with my mare and I stopped her and the others including the commander stopped with me.

"What is wrong, Queen?" the commander asked me.

"My mare Rosalina has a clog in her hoof. It's why when I rode her this time it felt off. We must rest her or at least send two of our soldiers back with her we can walk the rest of the way."

They all looked at me then their commander and we all waited. "Okay, we will let her rest but you are the only one who will clean her hoof so my men can take her back." I sighed with relief and patted my knee as a sign for her to lift her left front leg so I can clean it as much as I could.

Once I was done with her hoof and cleaned it as much as I could I gave her a final pat on the neck. "My sweet girl, you have served me well. Now I must let you rest till I return. We wasted so much time." Rosalina snorted as in protest, but I took what I needed from her saddle and set off on foot with the commander on his black war horse.

The journey was long and tiring, but we had one day left till we make it to the sea elves. I sat at the fire eating bread and cheese as I had to think about how to speak to the sea elves. Hell, who knows if the sea elves speak my human tongue or the forest elves' tongue. Maybe they don't speak at all and they just used hand gestures.

We won't know till we make it there to see for ourselves. I hope they can accept a human visiting them even if I am from the prophecy or not. Laying back on the ground, I stared at the night sky looking at the stars as I thought of ways to convince the sea elves to be prepared to fight on their home turf. After long, deep thoughts I fell deep asleep.

By late morning we made it to our destination and we were in luck. The sea elves were at the docks preparing to trade and set out to sea and trade amongst themselves or with humans. Who knows what happens to them after forest and sea elves have completed their trades. I looked at the commander and spoke calmly, "Commander, stay close but far away enough where we don't cause them any reason to think we came here to fight them." I watched the commander hesitate then nod and wait for me to be far enough ahead that he is nearby in case trouble came from them.

In my time with the forest elves, I had learned to speak what I needed in their language to get by. I spoke the forest elves' language loud enough so that the sea elves could hear me amongst the hustle and bustle here.

"I am here to seek an audience with the leader of the sea elves."

Everyone here stopped what they were doing to look at me and I heard gasps and whispers. I waited for what felt like an eternity until a female sea elf came down the ship laughing.

"We speak your native tongue, youngling. No need to try so hard to impress us."

I sighed with relief and stared at her with the courage I had when I faced to save the kids and in battle. "Sea elf leader —-"

"Call me Captain Zora young one." I bowed. "Yes, Captain Zora. I am Lynn, and I have come to seek your help on behalf of King Sebastian."

She gave me a look of shock then tilted her head. "So the forest elf king came to me for help. What for?" I shook my head. "My apologies for not clarifying. I meant that I asked to come here after hearing about you and your armada thinking you could be prepared for a possible battle out on the sea." She straightened her head and shook her head in refusal to help.

"Please, Captain Zora. We need your help to be prepared for all possible outcomes of a next battle site." I was sounding pathetic. Well I do not care. I will do anything to convince her to help us succeed against Asmodeus.

"What is in it for me then, youngling?" She, I had learned would not do anything without being paid for something equal for her services.

"Whatever you want from me you shall have. Anything to have you help us win against Asmodeus."

She stiffened at the name and I could tell she knew him well. Out of curiosity I had to ask to get more info on our ancient king. "Captain Zora, you knew him. May I ask how you knew about him?"

She looked saddened as if thinking about it pained her, but that sadness disappeared as soon as it came. "He and I were once lovers before his parents' murder and before he was exiled hundreds of years ago."

I was shocked to learn of this. But it gave me a bit more insight on our enemy. "Lynn, no price can be named just that you must be the one to kill him. I know the prophecy, and you are a future queen of a village that will become a kingdom after we win. Sebastian I already know has a desire to finish the job, but one part of the prophecy says that the future king or queen must be the one to defeat an ancient evil before this evil can continue to torment innocent souls."

I waved my goodbyes with hugs to the sea elves knowing they got our backs and has decided to trade for what they can and rotate in order to be prepared for the next battle even if it turns out to not be out on the waters yet.

On the trail leading back to Lorali I followed the sounds of a nearby stream to clean off any dirt on my body so I could be close to being presentable when I returned to the King's side. I was humming till I heard some rustling noises behind me and I froze then turned around.

"Come out and get dressed, little lady, or we will deliver you to King Wolf dead if we have to."

A soldier that belongs to King Asmodeus gave me a look of greed and lust. I felt so violated with that stare, but when I found my voice I sounded more calm than I felt.

"I will follow your demands only if you and your companion who is hiding will swear on your lives that you will have your backs turned to me as I get out to get dressed."

The leader of the two turned his head to his right and gave a curt nod then I saw them both turned their backs to me. I quickly got out and got my clothes back on and tried to search for my dagger I had carried with me in case I left or lost my sword in battle, but I learned as I saw it in the soldier's pocket that he thought ahead. I am utterly defenseless to the point where I can't even take down two men barehanded on my own even if I tried.

"Alright, pigs. You may take me to your devil King. No promises that I will bow to that evil man," I said with bitterness.

I was immediately backhanded and I fell to my knees, and soon I was dragged to my feet. Hands tied and mouth gagged. The gagging was to make sure I kept my mouth shut before I ended up dead. Hopefully the marks I left in the shore line area where I fell from the hit will help the commander have leads as to where I will be heading and luckily not on my own free will.

I pray that Sebastian can find me soon before this war ends because I will need to help fight all possible battles before I am dead because if the cities and the lands are not free from Asmodeus and his army then we will be dead for nothing. I may end up killing the king the cowardly way by being in his castle walls and read books about poison or something.

I will end his life before he ends a thousand more. I do not care if I am wounded or get bones broken in the process. It will all be worth it because Asmodeus will be dead. I will have fulfilled the prophecy if he dies at my hands. *Get ready Asmodeus, your reign will end here soon even if it is the last thing I will ever do.*

Chapter 10

I already know where they will put me since I have been captured. It wasn't long until they threw me into a cell that smelled of feces and vomit. "Have a nice time, princess," the tall but more feminine looking one said. The men both laughed like it was a joke, and I just rolled my eyes as they walked away chatting about something else now since their job with me was over.

Ugh! I should have waited to come home for a nice bath but no! My dumbass self wanted to feel a bit cleaner on the way back! I sat on a pile of clean straw to think about what the King needed me for. I hope the commander took note of where I was last and sped back home to tell Sebastian, but I hope Sebastian doesn't come for me first without making sure the King's soldiers from any new battlefield have been terminated.

It was dark when I heard the dungeon doors open and in came the King himself at my cell looking smug as if he won a huge prize. I turned my head to not look at him because if I do I will end up retching over his nice shoes. "Leave us." I turned my head to watch the soldiers and guards leave us alone. I felt cold to the bone and my face was pale. "So, princess, tell me your battle plans. If you don't I will summon my guards to hold you and whip you until you tell me." I gave him the nastiest glare and growled out, "I rather die than tell any of our plans to you ugly pig!"

His smirk disappeared and he called in his guards and told them to rip open my shirt and hold me as the other whipped my back till I bled and admit our plans. When the first whip hit, I screamed in pain, but the next one did not come yet.

"What are your battle plans!"

"Go to hell!"

At that he told them to do it again. He told them to keep whipping me until my back was covered in marks and bloodied cuts and I was unable to stand.

My voice hoarse and my back feeling wet from sweat or my blood I do not know. But I was glad when they were done and left me in my cell. I am a champ at keeping my mouth shut this long. Pretty sure Sebastian would have a coronary if he saw my bloodied back.

I was asleep on the bed without my back touching the straw because that would bring more pain. I was woken up a few minutes later to a man my age but who was a soldier and I sat up ready to fight him. "What does the soldier of my enemy want?" I said it with so much bitterness the man didn't seemed fazed by it.

"I came to give you some food and check your back for infections," he said kindly.

I felt cautious, but I showed my back in order for it to be looked at before I decide to eat whatever has been brought to me. The king doesn't want me dead yet so he sent one of his medical soldiers to check my back and feed me.

Back bandaged and staring at the bowl of soup I think about it. I do not know if he poisoned it. He needs me to find out our battle plans but once my use was up he will kill me like he did with my parents. I chose to eat it due to the fact that he will need me because he won't get answers from a dead woman.

"Leave me alone now, soldier, because your job here was accomplished."

I heard him heave a sigh and watched him leave. Next came in the King and the same soldiers who held me and caused me pain in my back. The soldiers brought in a whipping post this time. I am guessing they didn't have time the first round to bring it. With a nod to them they grabbed me and I never planned to struggle so they chained me to the post and got me ready for the whip all over again.

"What are your battle plans, Lynn?"

I laughed. "As fucking if I would tell you. So I do not know because we are still planning your next attack King Wolf."

Then came the whip and I yelped in pain. "I ask again, what are your plans!" "If I knew them now I wouldn't tell a disgusting fat pig like you!" That triggered him to get angry which was bad news for me, he might whip me till I am dead. With each hit on my back I screamed in pain until I was so numb from the pain and my voice so hoarse I couldn't even speak or say a damn thing anymore.

"I guess you had enough for today, princess. We will come back in two days in order to get more answers from you." Then he left with his soldiers trailing behind him.

I wept from pain and from homesickness. Then I heard some grunts and metal falling to the ground then I heard Sebastian's voice and I sat up eager to see with my own eyes. I hope I wasn't hallucinating him saving me right now. Then he came in under the cover of darkness but luckily I can see him with some light from the torches and I wept from joy at seeing him again. "Oh, Sebastian, I am so glad to see you again."

He grabbed the keys to the cells and found mine and unlocked my cell door and grabbed me into an embrace and there we stood holding onto each other like our life depended on it. When he tried to touch my back without knowing I gasped in pain and he shoved me at arms length. "You okay?" He was so concerned and I nodded. "Sebastian, let us leave while we still can because this is our only chance to come home alive." He agreed and grabbed my hand and like that we ran under the cover of darkness.

When the morning sun rose, we were finally back home and I was so exhausted and in pain and grimy that I do not care how many elves stared at us I was glad to finally be home for once. I was still dragged by him to his bed chamber and he helped me get clean and ready for bed.

"Fenri! Go get our healer and have her take a look at our future queen's back." Fenri nodded and bowed and left the room quickly.

"Sebastian, I am so tired. Can she look at my back tomorrow when I am not gonna pass out here?"

He shook his head no and he showered my face in

kisses like he was trying to make sure I was here alive and real. Well of course I am real, he wouldn't have dragged me for hours back home on the run if I was.

"When commander Green told me you were taken by Asmodeus's soldiers I thought my heart stopped and died right on the floor of the war room."

Hearing his confession shocked me and I kissed him deeply trying to reassure him that I am here and alive. I felt bad for not trying to put up a fight, but what choice did I have against two armed men while I had nothing to use since they took my dagger.

"Sebastian, I am here and alive. If you never came he would have killed me anyways. He wanted to know our battle plans which I was lucky enough to know nothing of for now. If I told him he will kill me anyways since he will not have any use for me anymore."

He held me tightly until the female healer came in and shoved him away from me to get better access to my back. I laughed at the fake hurt in his eyes when he was shoved away from me but gave me a wink and said he is going to make some final plans on our next battle.

"Lady Lynn, you could have tried to fight your way back here you know instead of letting them take you so I can witness this."

"I know, but I had no way of success if there were two against one and one is unarmed. The king will be furious once he finds out I am missing from my cell."

She nodded in agreement because who wouldn't get upset if their prisoner escaped from their cell? After a few minutes of cleaning and bandaging my back, I was told to rest, which we all know I won't do since I want to keep my skills sharp. For today though I will sleep since I sat in the cell for twenty-four hours or so without any sleep. Waiting to get tortured into spilling the plans Sebastian has.

I fell deep asleep where I am temporarily safe and can finally return to the real world later strong and ready to take down armies. I was awakened a bit to the sound of Sebastian coming in to bathe for bed and felt him crawl in bed next to me but I was still too exhausted to say anything so I fell deep asleep all over again.

Chapter 11

I was already awake and ready to train and follow any orders given to me for our next battle. I was sparring with the commander who helped me get rescued by Sebastian and he was giving me tips here and there on how to avoid this attack and another and we practiced it immediately after it was said. Once we were done with tips to prevent different attacks, my wounds reopened and I gasped in pain and blood slowly oozed out of my back.

"We are done here, my Queen, you have reopened your wounds and can't keep going if you will black out."

"I will not stop because of a scratch. I will train to keep up with you all in battle so I am not letting you all take on my part of the fight."

I saw him hesitate, obviously thinking about Sebastian and what he would say to the commander if he saw us training with my back bleeding. Then he nodded and was waiting for me to make the first move. I am glad he is going to let me continue till I say "no more". But before I could try anything, Sebastian came to me immediately and held me back. Commander nodded and left me and the angry Sebastian alone.

"You will not train in this condition till your back is

healed completely."

"I must train to keep up with you all so I am not the only human lagging."

"Lynn, there will be plenty of time for that since we haven't seen from our spies the next battlefield. Nor has the sea elves so we are safe to rest and heal while we can for now."

At that I sagged and passed out in his arms, and I knew he won't let me fall to the ground. I was on an empty battlefield. On the other side of the field is Asmodeus. His own soldiers don't know his true name, but those who have seen him from hundreds of years ago. Sebastian is not here with me so it is true that only I can kill the evil King that has plagued this world.

I got ready and he just stood there mocking me with only a smile. I charged after him, and he blocked my attack with his own sword. Then, dead soldiers appeared all around us. The field is soaked in their blood. Next I saw was Sebastian's body and that stopped me from what I was doing and soon I felt cold metal in my chest.

I woke up gasping and screaming for Sebastian and he burst through his bedchamber doors and held me tightly. Rocking and soothing my tremors. Once I was calm, I asked him, "What is the time?" "It is already night and it's still summer." I laughed at that last part. "Okay, I can already tell it is still that time of year due to the humidity this whole place has." He laughed with me and I felt loads better.

I got out of bed while he was asleep and went outside on the balcony to think and plan our future. "Hello, Queen." I was startled and I grabbed my dagger and looked at the stranger sitting on the stone railing next to me. "Who are you?" I asked with caution. "I am hurt that the Queen forgot who I am after we met after she saved those kids."

"Hermes!" I was in shock.

"You are an elf?"

"I thought you could tell that I was no ordinary wolf?"

I shook my head and apologized. "I believe you look way better in your wolf form than your elf form." He only shrugged. Then he transformed back to a wolf that I am used to seeing. *Is this better Queen?* I was shocked at hearing that voice and I looked around to find out how fake this was. *Do not keep looking for something that is already in front of you. I am using telepathy to talk to you.*

I looked at him and nodded in understanding then held my hand out to him and he licked it and moved to have my hand on his head and I pet him smiling. "I like this side of you a lot, Hermes." *Would you like it better if I was a perverted elf?* I glare at him.

"Sebastian or I would have you skinned alive if you decided to be that kind of person."

I was only joking Queen. And besides, I have a mate, she is all I ever need in my lifetime. I smiled and thought that I would not live as long as Sebastian because I am a human and elves live for a long time past the year of one-hundred. I continued to pet the gray-haired wolf as I stared out into the night in deep thought about what would happen to me once everything is said and done.

Morning came and I was well rested even though I

came back to bed late than usual. I decided to head to the kitchens and see if they will allow me to help knead dough or basically anything while I am unable to train with my wounds on my back being a major concern for Sebastian.

I was lucky enough to help knead dough for our morning bread and once that was done they allowed me to watch them on how they bake and prepare a fresh batch for tomorrow. I had loads of fun because I remember my kitchen staff back in Estonia used to let my mother and I watch and help them make bread and any other foods that we see when we have breakfast.

The memory saddened me, but I didn't let it linger because even without my parents I can still come back to the kitchens whenever I want and have the same feelings as before. I helped serve Sebastian's first then the others then I was commanded to go back to my room with Sebastian so they can serve me since I am royalty. Not really wanting to make them feel like they are using me, I do as they asked and returned to Sebastian who chuckled and that was a sign he knew why I was back here.

"My staff sent you back here so they can feed you?"

I nodded and sat on the bed next to him. He chuckled and stood and kissed the top of my head then left for kingly duties. Next, after he left, the servants brought me my breakfast and I smiled. "Thank you for this when I won't mind skipping one breakfast." I got a dagger glare from Helda and I surrendered to eating a late morning breakfast.

Late this morning I put on my riding clothes and

took my Rosalina for a ride. About an hour later, Sebastian was out with us on his horse and we rode for awhile until we came by a stream and had a picnic there. Only because I never had the lunch planned like him, but it was romantic.

After lunch we watched the stream flow by calmly and peacefully. Rose nudged my shoulder and I smiled at her and pet her nose then fed her a peppermint, her favorite treat out of many.

"Needy girl. I hope you don't beg for these treats so often because I will train you to earn them."

She snorted in protest and Sebastian, and I laughed then she left to graze next to her friend Thunder. Once it was dark, I helped Sebastian pack up the picnic. Next we hopped onto our horses backs and rode back to the castle to get cleaned up for our evening meal and to hear from him what news he has for me.

Back at the castle I cleaned up for the evening meal including being ready for a serious conversation for any updates on the army from Asmodeus. I even just remembered why he couldn't have tried to find us from the beginning because he lived here so he should remember where his old home was but if he hasn't done it yet it means his mind was erased if he was banished from his own home he remembers everything else but not the location.

I smile at the thought but realized he is only gonna keep fighting until we are outnumbered and exhausted, weak to the point we can't keep going and end up dying. I tried to keep thinking like Asmodeus but hearing about who he was and what changed him isn't enough to be him where we can figure out his next move. But pretty sure Sebastian knows his way of thinking better than anyone. I am glad I can help prepare for open sea battle but it isn't enough to get to him in person and we are at a point where one day I have to kill him so I must train to keep up with even the oldest elf who pretends to be human and changes his looks over the years but kept the name.

"Lynn, my spies have reported that Asmodeus and his second set of army hasn't been sent out yet so we have time and you are hopefully healed enough where we can train you for stamina."

I nodded grateful, because I need to keep up with the elves in a battle and if I get exhausted that will be my downfall but if Sebastian was with me he would have tagged in to try and catch up with him. Not in a good way though and I hope he doesn't get to distracted from the moment where he gets killed.

"Sebastian, when the time comes where me and you have to face Asmodeus head on. I beg of you to never get distracted from the past. It will be your downfall. When I am rested enough to fight Asmodeus one on one you must go help the others and do your best to sense when you should tag back in to help me find a weak spot to kill him."

He looked at me shocked but I only gave him my serious look because this all has to end soon and he knows it has to end. He looks defeated but nods as a sign he understands.

"Lynn, I do not want to lose you. I wished the prophecy said I had to kill him not you."

"I know you do, Sebastian. I love you for wanting to keep me away from the hardest battle, but I must complete it. No one but me can complete this prophecy." My heart softened at his attempt to protect me out of love.

"Lynn, I will do whatever it takes to keep you alive in battle then."

Smiling I said, "And I you because how the hell are we gonna have kids for heirs to the throne if you are not here? And your kingdom will blame me for your death."

"They won't, and I did get word from you home in Estonia. My advisors tell me everything is going smoothly. But Argos is not acting completely like me."

I laughed and was surprised because if Argos sounds like he is acting like Sebastian after being around me for so long. He tilted his head confused as to what I was laughing at and I shook my head trying to help him understand.

"Sebastian, he is acting like you perfectly fine because, the longer you are with me the more open and nicer you are around me."

He looked at me then smiled and laughed with me completely understanding what I meant. "Okay point taken."

"Told you Sebastian besides it is a good thing but we will keep your true origin a secret so you will have to be disguised as a human when I return from battle to let my people know the results of the tyrant king."

"I know but, Lynn, you are a bright light that shines with positivity and calmness. If you are gone so is the light and we would have to find a way to tell your people what happened to you."

"I know, but nothing will happen to me because we got each other's back."

Chapter 12

It has been a few weeks since the first battle I was in. It was already fall, and I was honored to be at the births of some elves since their husbands have passed or are busy with Sebastian getting trained and planning for any possible attack on a new village, battlefield, or us.

I experienced only three births, and it has already got me to wishing for some of my own already, but I knew deep down we couldn't have any until we were officially married and this war was over.

"Queen Lynn!"

I was confused as to why I was being called, but Fenri came running to me and oddly not out of breath. I waited for him to get closer so he could tell me where I was needed now or what he has to tell me.

" King Sebastian has said he wanted you and him to be married tomorrow at sunset."

I was shocked and excited and asked him where I should go to help get everything prepared. Fenri only smiled and said to be in my room and he would have Sebastian's mother's old wedding gown brought to me. Then my female servants would work together to have the gown fit to my size. I then remembered that I am shorter than a female elf and pretty sure they are close to five foot ten. I am sadly five foot four.

I rushed to my room to wait with my female servants to have a dress fitting. I prayed that my height won't cause so much of an issue with altering the dress to fit me.

It took all evening to make the dress a perfect fit to my body. Next I told them how I prefer my hair to be and asked them to manage it like that while also making my hair look beautiful for the wedding. Even doing that took all night because we had so many hairstyles to try and figure out which suited me best with the gown from his mother. Exhausted and my head hurting from the strains of so many styles I crawled into bed to sleep for the big day tomorrow.

Getting ready in the dress that his mother wore for her wedding and I cannot wait for when this war is over and when Sebastian and I have heirs and that one of them would be a girl so we could make this dress a tradition for the women in this new family to wear for their wedding until they have a different taste.

I was nervous but excited at the same time so I kept telling myself to take deep breaths. I was spoken to by Helda who doesn't know me well, but I knew she would say something to keep me positive.

"I know if your parents were here they would be proud of the woman who you came to be."

I teared up and hugged the elf woman thanking her. Then Fenri came in and stood there looking at me. I tilted my head confused and requested him to tell me what he needed to say to me. Cheeks obviously flushed, he came to tell me it is time to go to the throne room to have our union.

I smiled and had Fenri lead the way so I could stand next to Sebastian to become one with him. As soon as he and the whole room saw me, they all looked shocked and the men flushed, but their own mates seemed to give their men the death glare if they chose to rush to me, which I highly doubt.

Finally married, we chose to spend tonight in his bedchamber and we talked about if we should try to have heirs soon. It's the only thing we talked about because who knows if we would survive this final battle and we would need our kids to succeed after us.

"Sebastian, we should ask your main advisor about this because we do know we need successors if we die even if they are only babes we still have Fenri to be in charge until they are of age, but it is best to check in with him and see what he says about this."

Sebasian called in Fenri and asked him the question he and I had struggled solving for hours. Then, he gave us the answer that deep down we knew it had to happen. But Fenri had more to say so we encouraged him to tell us what is wrong.

"My King and my Queen, the next battle is on the sea. We heard from Captain Zora about the ships Asmodeus has sent out there to destroy us immediately."

Shocked, we had our servants get us dressed for battle so we could ride out to the docks with our soldiers and fight Asmodeus's men. The children will have to wait because, this, is more important and I'm pretty sure we will have kids after Asmodeus is dead. When I voiced my thoughts to Sebastian, he seemed to relax a little bit and kissed me long and deeply. That is a sign we have hope to fight harder and survive this battle and the final one hopefully against Asmodeus.

Chapter 13

In gear we wait with Captain Zora to have her tell us when is the right time to engage with the enemy. Sebastian is a king as I am a queen. You would think we would be the one's commanding the armada, but no, this is not our specialty in gauging the waters like it has been for centuries for the sea elves.

Captain Zora pulled me to the side and told me the plans she had made for me even though Sebastian would hate it. I was thrilled to be quite honest to do this because it means I can help more than he thinks I can. The plan is to stall the main enemy ship and get me on board and to rig anything that causes it to move and to steal any battle plans so the enemy can't use it to refer to in the future temporarily. Next they plan to keep them stalled while I sneak on-board and hide the plans somewhere in a secret compartment only she will know and it is a good thing. Less we know where things we take for us are hidden by her the more successful we will be in this battle.

Midday, and the battle on the sea began far from the docks where the innocents live. I cut through my enemies while Sebastian and the others had kept them busy far away from me while I snuck onto the main ship.

At least, I hoped this ship that came to us was the main one.

After a few minutes of searching the cabins for the battle plans and the rooms that propel this huge ship I was lucky to find it unguarded. It was too easy, and I then knew it was a trap as soon as arrows whizzed by my head leaving a scratch on my cheek. I had an intake of breath due to the shock of newness of a new pain. Who knew I would be a bit more sensitive to pain on my face?

It doesn't matter though because this plan of going in and out failed. Sebastian will know I am not near him like I promised I would before this all began. I should not rely on him because it is my destiny to defeat Asmodeus so this is the practice of independence in a battle that I need. Well, mostly since these are not elves only humans, I can take them down in no time compared to hundred- year- old elves.

I parried off an attack to my legs. Sounds of metal against metal clanging were too loud, but I had to drown it out in order to stay alive and return to the others soon as possible. I managed to get two down, but in this small space more kept popping out of nowhere and it made no sense so I reached out with my mind to find Hermes and beg him to find Sebastian and work on finding the secret passageway on this ship to the room I was in.

My Queen, I have found your mate, King Sebastian. We are on our way to you as we locate where the men you are fighting is coming from.

I sighed in relief for hope was on the way to staunch the waves of the oncoming soldiers. Archers killed, now the room is being filled with the bodies of soldiers while also being flooded with the blood from their bodies. I grabbed the parchment of the plans and lucked out that I already killed the propellers of the ship I ran out to meet Hermes in his natural wolf form and Sebastian covered in blood.

Not quite sure whose, but we must sink this ship and work our way to the others so they don't come to help this main one. We never stopped taking down each soldier coming at us. I am already back with more wounds than I can count this time but none too fatal. More like scratches. which is a good thing because I am not ready to end my own story just yet.

"Sebastian! Hermes! We must sink the ship before we get off completely."

They understood exactly what I had planned so we poked a few holes at the base of the ship then raced to the deck to get off and back onto our own ship. I was caught on a fallen beam of the ship and I was close to being drowned with the sinking ship if Hermes my favorite wolf did not use his huge paws to break the beam into more pieces in order for me to get free.

Back on our main ship that Captain Zora commands, we noticed the other ships around us were no longer. Here it was like they retreated. I felt my whole body go rigid and face turn pale.

"Not good. Not good at all."

"Lynn, what is wrong? We won this battle quickly and they ran away."

"I know, but this retreat was instant. The first time was not a quick retreat," I said as I turned to Sebastian.

"Sebastian, you should know these guys left for a reason not to save themselves but because they collected something that they were sent to do by the demands of Asmodeus."

I saw a bulb turn on in his head and then he too felt what I felt, dread by what they could have taken. He shouted orders and told Captain Zora to have her crew search all their own ships for what has been stolen that the king has been needing. All of a sudden a scorching pain was emanating from my side, and we saw green vine-like lines coming out of a wound that must have happened when I was fighting against waves of soldiers in that cabin.

Sebastian was white as a sheet and we knew I was poisoned. That is when I fell to the ground. Sebastian held my head in his lap as the elves of all kinds surrounded me trying to see what they could do to heal me so I could live for another day.

"Lynn, everyone has ideas on what that poison is and all are looking and finding antidotes to heal you so don't give in to this evil poison."

I smirked. "Love as if! I have a duty to attend to so I will fight this in order to help the healers cure me."

I coughed and started to pant. I must fight to stay awake as I was forced to try all the cures that were made and all said that what they made would never affect me badly after the previous cure given to me. That is a good thing. That means whichever cure was given to me would end up being the cure. But, in order to figure which it was, we tried each one every few hours to test which one was the cure.

Chapter 14

I was in and out of consciousness. Hallucinating that I was alone and freaking out until the healers used magic or medicine to sedate me where I am calm and back in reality. The last cure I was given was some sort of blue liquid. We are playing the waiting game.

It feels like it has been years since the sea battle. I could only hear once in a while the conversation others had with Sebastian while I hear his voice fraught with worry for me to live. I am doing my best to fight. He needs to keep this battle going until I am fully healed.

By night on whatever day it was since the battle, I was feeling a little better. I was moving around the room and stretching doing the things I usually do. Sebastian came in first and kissed me deeply as he held me tightly.

"Can't. . . . breathe, Sebastian."

"Sorry, my love."

He suddenly loosened his hold on me, and I took a deep breath of air so I could feel alive more or once again. I held his face in my hands as I smiled. He leaned his face into my hands as he closed his eyes. He was worried about me, scared for me. I am glad I got to marry him.

Wait, Estonia won't know we were married so this

is step one of being together. Well now I know we have to get married outside the mansion I lived in to get married in front of my own people. At least I got my mother's wedding gown saved somewhere in the mansion.

"What are you thinking, love?"

I smiled. "Nothing of importance."

He smiled to accept that I wouldn't talk about the lesser things. He rushed to look outside our doors, left first then right. Next he shut and locked our doors and rushed to me kissing my neck lightly, and my heart began to beat faster.

I know now he wanted to make love to me but not have kids just yet. He slowly kissed down my neck then he rushed in taking his tunic and trousers off. I stood there blushing like a fool unable to get used to the last time we did it.

Once he was completely naked, he lifted me up and slowly laid me down on our bed kissing me deeply. He softly caressed me with his hands as his hands went up my legs to my breasts. I bit my lip trying to take in this moment so I could remember it until I die.

He was on top of me, and I could already tell his heart was beating just as fast as mine. I moaned as I felt him shove himself in me. This pleasure will never get old to be honest. He started moving in and out of me slowly making my moans soft; then he kissed me as he slowly picked up speed making me moan louder against his soft lips.

His hands squeezed and caressed my breasts. I can feel all the callouses and it makes the caress even better and erotic. I moaned so loud it felt like the others could hear us, but I did not care. I felt like the seams inside me were about to come undone if he kept going.

He thrust harder and faster and that was my undoing. I came so hard that it felt like it was part of my energy. As I came he came in me as well.

Taken the sea bane so as to not have kids so soon before the war is over. We laid in each other's arms for a long while taking in each other's scent and feel of the other's body to memory in case that anything happened to the other we could remember this day.

Chapter 15

Today is normal, no more battles we have to face just yet so we are doing chores and keeping ourselves fit and prepared for battle. I walked around Lorali to see if I missed anything on my quick tour with Fenri. As I was walking around, the elves of this kingdom kept looking at me for some reason.

I called for Fenri when I was back inside the castle to ask him about the stares I was getting now from the others.

"Well, not to be inappropriate, my Queen, but they are staring at your beauty."

I blinked at him confused. "Huh?"

"My Queen, you have gotten very beautiful since you have been in our kingdom and the change over the past few weeks has made you look more flawless."

I was even more confused as he kept telling me something that somehow keeps sounding so foreign to me. Instead of letting it sit there for me to keep thinking about it, I just accepted the words being told and walked to the stables to go riding in the surrounding woods with Rosalina.

In my brown riding outfit, I hopped into the saddle and spurred Rosalina to the trail made long ago when the elves first settled here in Eros. I just rode till

Rosalina got tired and we made a stop a mile away from Lorali, but the smell of salt water was close so we were near the sea. Ceres Sea, the sea where we fought our second battle. I left Rose at the edge of the woods so I could walk on the beach of Ceres.

I was walking alongside the water until I found a smooth stone and it shined as bright as the sun. Curious about what it truly was I picked it up to observe it and I knocked on it because the size and shape was unlike any other common stone I had seen. The sound was not a sound a stone should make. Stones are solid, and this stone could never be what I had feared it was. I studied the stone a bit and noticed the color was of a dark purple almost black.

"This is not a stone. I had heard of these kinds of stories. This is a dragon's egg."

I was shocked and afraid and looked around the area to see if there were more, but this one is the last of its kind or the last to my knowledge since no one knew what happened to the dragons or the elves and humans before my time who once existed. Some say they left Eros to other lands beyond the sea.

Others say, they went up against Asmodeus but all died because none could defeat him. To be honest, I am learning so much including hearing tales like this since my stay here in Lorali. I wished my race knew about this and told everyone in Estonia so I could learn and have some hopes about this.

I debated on bringing it back home to show Sebastian or not. *If I brought this back pretty sure they would be searching for more of these eggs, which I doubt anyone will succeed because no one knows where the others of this race are.* I finally decided to raise this dragon alone in secret even though I had duties to take care of, but part of me thinks I can defeat Asmodeus with the strength of a dragon.

"Why do you have that egg, Queen?"

"Hermes, do not speak a word of this to anyone because trust me, if you all started to look for more of these eggs you wouldn't find any because I already looked. I have a feeling this one dragon will help me fight Asmodeus."

I looked at my wolf companion, and he gave me the look of hesitation but bowed his head.

"As you wish my Queen, did you wish me to send word that you will be camping out here for awhile?"

I smiled and nodded. Not truly surprised he knew my plans in figuring this out. "Hermes, feel free to return with fresh meat in case this little one hatches and I can't go out hunting immediately." With that he transformed into a big silver wolf and took off back to Lorali to send word and bring back what I had asked.

It was dark, and I had a fire on the beach going as I studied the egg for awhile and thinking about all the stories and legends told about elves and humans having a special bond with dragons to the point it's called dragon riders. No story mentioned magic or anything else. So I have to learn things on my own. I was thinking on how this dragon could help us succeed if in the past they possibly failed.

I woke up sleeping against Rosalina and the egg already hatched and it squeaking at me. I was shocked and smiled and held out my hand to let it trust me first. The small purple dragon hesitated and snorted smoke, then it touched my palm, and a jolt of cold electricity went up my arm and all I could do was gasp in pain so I fell and blacked out.

I awoke for a second time and saw it was noon and there was a mark on my right palm where there shouldn't be. It was a shape of a rose. It was an odd mark, but I was more worried for the little dragon and I looked around for him or her.

"Little dragon? Where are you?"

I heard a squeak and I was relieved that it was eating what Hermes brought back. "Thank you, Hermes, I am also not gonna ask why you are not afraid of this dragon."

"My Queen, I was there when dragons and humans bonded."

Now that was a shock. He must be way older than Sebastian. This gives me so many questions and it may help me succeed in my prophecy.

"Hermes, tell me everything you know about these bonds we and the dragons had."

"The insignia on your palm is gonna be different for all the riders."

That confused me, and I waited for him to clarify what he meant by it. "I mean, for example, one rider has an insignia of a tree alive or dead depends on the relations of the rider. One would have an insignia of the sun or a moon."

That explains it, but what do the insignias truly mean? I didn't ask because it would have to be something I have to solve on my own with my dragon.

"My Queen, dragons and their riders will have mind melds where they can read and speak into each others minds. Dragons have magic, but they don't even know what they can truly do besides breathe fire, fly, and hunt like a hunter."

"So it also means once a rider is born they have magic in their blood?"

He nodded, and I could not help but ask him as I loved on my hatched dragon, "So is the magic self taught? Or the oldest magic user or rider teaches the younger generation how to control and use it?"

"There is always a teacher to teach the younglings how to hone their skills."

That brought me to my last feared question where I knew the obvious answer but I needed it confirmed. "So that means there are no more original teachers who can teach me?" He nodded and I sighed.

"Well can you teach me the most basic ones or at least ones you can remember?"

I saw him tilt his head to think about it then he nodded. "I will teach you and your dragon what I remember but only once your dragon and you are already mind melded together."

I smiled and nodded as I fed another chunk of raw meat to my dragon. I will have to let Rose watch it until I return with a good amount of meat to last until it can hunt on its own.

Chapter 16

A week later the baby dragon had gotten bigger. It was the size of a house cat. I even tried to teach it how to fly. I wished to know what gender it is. I knew it should get used to flying soon and it should also learn to hunt on its own.

Once it was flying the next day, it flew up so high into the clouds I had assumed it was never going to return. But it was a cloudy day. There should not be any storms today but there was thunder and lightning then out came my dragon, fully grown and bigger than a home. I soon felt an unfamiliar touch to my mind and let it enter, but it was masculine and deep.

"Hello, Little One."

I was shocked and was happy at the same time. "Hello, dragon. I assume you need a name?" He blinked and bowed his head as a sign as a yes. I took a good look at him as I thought about it.

"Your name shall be Aegeus."

I heard rather than felt him hum in pleasure and it made me smile. Then Hermes came and waited for me to give him permission to train me in the basics of magic.

I nodded to him, and we then started to train with our minds until Aegeus and I were too tired to think and concentrate with each other's different teachings. Around dusk Sebastian appeared. I was startled, and Aegeus was growling protectively and I stood between them so both didn't start to fight.

"Aegeus, meet my husband, King Sebastain of Lorali. Sebastian meet my dragon and our hope against Asmodeus; Aegeus."

Aegeus stopped growling and spoke in my head to get to my husband, *Well met, Elf King.* "Well met, sharp fang," said my husband. I relaxed and I finally told him the week that I found Aegeus to now.

"Well, I can train you in magic, my Queen, while Hermes trains Aegeus in his flight and later on fire breath."

I thought long and hard about it while consulting about the challenges and how it may help us succeed with our training with Aegeus. *Little One, I must say it can help us a great deal to strengthen our mental bond so we both can teach the other what we have learned. The demon king will not start another battle unless he has to.*

So let the wolf elf train me from what he has seen before our time and let your mate train you in the arts that have existed for a millenia. I smiled and nodded to Hermes and Sebastian. "Let our training begin."

We trained for hours in the elven language. Sebastian was very patient with me where I was not truly patient with myself. *Calm yourself, Little One. Once calm try again and therefore you shall succeed.* Listening to Aegeus, I became calm and collected then tried to raise a pebble in my hand again.

The pebble rose a few inches off my marked palm to the point it took too much energy and I was already sweating. We never spoke because we understood each other's boundaries into focusing on the task at hand.

Late into the morning Aegeus and I have repeated to Hermes and Sebastian what we both learned from the mind meld. We got praised by them both then I had to keep practicing the skills I was taught till Hermes has decided I had perfected it and was able to move on to a bit more advanced ones.

We were taking a break for lunch, and Fenri raced to me frantic and worried. "My Queen! We have an emergency there is soldiers coming here where you are located and the King has told me to warn you to get ready!"

He was panting and frozen wide-eyed as he looked at Aegeus. "Fenri, thank you, and the King will tell you all about this once you return to his side so he can come here to help." I saw his hesitation then he made the right choice to hurry on back to Sebastian's side. *Oh Aegeus, we haven't begun to make a saddle for you so I ride on you as your rider.*

He bent down to put his nose against my forehead. *I know, Little One, but we must make do by fighting from the sky and the ground.* I nodded and he moved to look down at me and I up at him. Then we waited with Hermes training us together in our next battle in a saddle made for dragons.

"My Queen, we had all different sized saddles for dragons in the ancient times so I have my shape shifting people bring it here so you and your dragon can fly and fight together."

Next thing we knew two elves brought in a saddle meant for dragons of Aegeus's size and they all taught me how to put it on while Aegeus also learned because we can not stop unless we are synchronized and we are made as one.

Once the saddle has been put on and after being told how to tie myself into the saddle so I do not fall off of Aegeus and to my own death, we took off to hover over where we were to gauge on our enemy forces.

Little One, I can see from a distance that our enemies won't be here till noon. We shall stay here to practice more from the elder shape shifter till it is time for my fangs and claws to destroy our enemies.

I laughed and spoke to him through his head, *Aegeus, I believe once they spotted you we would have already won without bloodshed to occur.* He snorted as smoke came through his nostrils. *Perhaps, but who knows how many will be brave to stand against a dragon and his rider?* Aegeus made a great point that I could not argue with.

We landed next to Hermes and we waited as we trained me in honing in on my swordsmanship. I took the time after my sparring with Hermes to scan the minds of small creatures like ants and rabbits. We stayed like that while waiting for Asmodeus's army to arrive so I can show off the hope for the whole of Eros.

Chapter 17

Time has come, and we are ready to test our bonds as rider and dragon for the very first time. I sat in his saddle, and we took off to fly over the soldiers so Aegeus can make himself known and be feared by the soldiers below.

Aegeus let out a resounding roar that startled the birds in the trees. We saw some soldiers drop their weapons and flee while most of the army stayed even though they might die by the fangs and claws of Aegeus. *Aegeus, you were right, most men will not back down until they win this fight with honor. Too bad the ones who fled will get kicked out and be put as civilians.*

He gave me a low rumble in his throat as a sign of satisfaction he was right. I smiled knowing we will have an interesting fight. We got into the fray while the soldiers elves from Lorali were arriving later.

I hopped off of Aegeus and swung my sword right and left felling each soldier that crossed my path. All the soldiers who faced me were brave men, but when it comes to being killed by Aegeus, all you could hear were their high-pitched screams turning them into cowards with zero honor.

Even when each soldier tried to take me from behind, either Aegeus or Sebastian was there before they could land an attack on me. I began to soak the sands of the beach in my enemies' blood. It is a sad way to end things, but all this bloodshed is necessary to win against Asmodeus.

This battle lasted into the night where we still had all our soldiers and our enemies left with only a dozen of their own. We stayed on the beach to gather ourselves before we headed back to Lorali. I pet Rosalina who raced towards me worried and soon very relaxed because I was there calming her.

Little One, this battle made us very lucky, but I can sense we have a lot more adventure soon. Something tells me we will have to leave your mate and the others behind so we can discover more about our destiny.

I sighed and nodded hating the fact it has to be true. *I know, Aegeus, but it will be hard for Sebastian to rule alone again while waiting for more signs of another battle. He and I have hopes of having heirs in order to keep our bloodline going.*

He nodded and touched his nose to my forehead out of love and understanding. I smiled softly. It is only a matter of time of when we are in need far away from Lorali.

We came back home with Hermes riding Rose while I sat upon Aegeus's back to get used to the feel of being on a creature bigger than a horse. Once we appeared back home, the elves of Lorali were shocked to see me and a dragon. Then Sebastian gathered their attention to introduce Aegeus's existence and about the new hope it brings to us here.

The elves cheered and tossed flowers of all kinds to

Aegeus, and it made me smile because I could sense at how uncomfortable it is for him. I hopped off Aegeus and ran to Sebastian to hug and kiss him then to whisper so only he could hear me, "Sebastian, Aegeus has told me that soon we shall leave Lorali to find others like us and train them if they exist in this era."

He frowned but nodded because we both know there is no other way to escape from this because we need to take every opportunity to defeat Asmodeus. And I hope it won't be after the festival for Aegeus.

"Tonight we shall celebrate the return of the dragons! A new age is soon to come!"

I smiled at Sebastian as the elves of Lorali cheered. At that moment I realized the time of leaving was approaching even if I did not want it to. I kept smiling in order to not scare the others so they didn't see my own fears. Sebastian talks of the celebration lasting for two days which means I will leave with Aegeus tomorrow making it seem like I never had been here for long even though it has been two months or so and it was almost winter.

We drank wine and ale while everyone played harps and made special presentations to show off who they are personally for Aegeus in honor of the return of dragons and of our future.

Little One, once we win this war, you and your mate, Elf King will have the time to have offspring.

I smiled and nodded at the hope of a family with Sebastian. And I listened to all the little elf children talking about their skills and how they would be in the kingdom once this war is over and when they are all old enough to work. I smiled and I was told to sing to the whole kingdom by an elf who could find the left out details of a person without being told by another source.

The whole kingdom was silent and looking at me patient and waiting while I sat stunned and shy. *Go on, Little One, we all wish to hear you sing.* I hesitated a bit, but I stood up and used simple magic to help everyone hear me as I sing.

"My home, my home, ohh I wished it was not in danger. Time has come, the prophecy that I must be the one to save the world. I wished this war never existed, it's too late, it has destroyed homes, families. Lands soaked in blood and screams. Time has come for me to help save the world and bring peace."

I sang for a few more minutes then I heard only silence after my singing stopped. Even Sebastian stared at me in silence, but I could tell he was tearing up moved. I felt shy because it is rare for me to sing at all.

We bade Sebastian a good night and I rushed back to our bedchamber to pack up some clothes for travel and food and weapons that I could hide on my body and carry openly. Once everything is packed, I leave a heartfelt note letting Sebastian know where Aegeus and I are going and what we are going to do.

Chapter 18

.

It is a cool morning on Aegeus's back. We have been in the air for hours since last night from the celebration of the return of the dragons. Luckily for me I have been reading in the royal library of the legends of the riders and their dragons. Our first stop to find them was where they all began before everyone in Eros divided and lives miles apart or even could be neighbors, who knows, but something in the old city of Ares must have details on their last recent whereabouts.

We heard screams from down below, and I told Aegeus to land near the village of Soma. As we landed, I hopped off brandishing my sword and starting to fight soldiers without trying to give away who I am and that I have a dragon with me.

Aegeus! Stay hidden. We must not reveal we are the dragon riders yet. We do not know who is on our side and who isn't.

Yes, Little One, but if you are in severe danger I will come and save you and risk revealing ourselves.

I smiled as I fought a soldier to my right pushing him back just in time for a soldier to my left to come at me. I dodged and swiped but somehow never got in a scratch until I finally realized Asmodeus used something that makes these soldiers much more different from last time. This is a cause for concern and something to investigate.

I got slashed in the leg due to my lack of focus on the now. Time for concern later. I parried each attack at my legs, my chest, and my head. One was losing stamina so I took my chance and stabbed him through the chest. *Ha! Not everyone is like the elves.* With hope and my sweat beading all over my body I began to find patterns with each soldier and wore them down enough to kill them.

It is high noon, and around me dead soldiers lay unmoving and I am surrounded by the villagers of Soma. I just pant, not caring for the thanks and cheers at me for saving them. I am super tired and sweaty. I scanned around the surroundings trying to figure out why Asmodeus's soldiers were sent here.

I went around and asked for reasons to why they came here. All said they came for taxes and if they could not pay the taxes their town would be burned to the ground. I was furious and it gave me more reason to hurry on this journey and defeat Asmodeus.

We left with more than we ever had packed for ourselves and we flew till it was too dark to see. We made camp along the Nora River close to the outskirts of the woods close to the desert area. We rested and drank lots of water to prepare ourselves to rest and travel in the hot sands where none have truly survived. We have no choice but to travel through it not around it.

It will take months for us to return with any hopes of finding more riders if we went around the Death

Sands. Aegeus is sound asleep, and I look up at the stars wishing this all never happened. Though if it weren't for all the bad events I wouldn't have married an elf king and met a lot of wonderful people and get to see a real dragon and more or less be a dragon rider.

By sunrise we are walking on foot through the Death s

Sands. How did it get its name? Pretty sure the word death says it all and all the animal bones half buried in the sands.

Even though it is winter, the Death Sands lives up to its reputation of it being scorching hot all year round and a bit cooler at night. I was glad we had more water skeins to hold our water while we got burns all over our bodies. Well, my body since Aegeus seems to not mind the heat and the sands blowing all over the place.

Once it was night, it was cooler than during the day. We drank and ate what we could to help us travel to the ruins of Latona. We have only two days left of being in the Death Sands according to the map of Eros. I studied it and started planning on how to get to the edge of the sands and closer to the ruins of Latona.

On Aegeus's back we flew all day and walked all night till we finally made it to our destination. It gave me a darker skin tone than I usually had, but it helps me blend in to other villages and cities.

"Aegeus, you must stay here in case this city still has people living here, at least ones who are not like us. I must find out alone."

If you find others like us, I will know to come to your side as to let the others know we are on the side of good.

I smiled and nodded then trekked alone with my own pack. It has been tiring, but I knew at the end of the journey it would be worth it.

By noon and after my rest and lunch, I finally made it to the city of Latona. At least, what is left of it. Keeping my senses on high alert, I walked through the stone gates that look like they have been blasted from the outside. Followed the cobblestone path to find homes burned to the ground and a tower here and there made for dragons that still stand, but it seems like six towers were destroyed like the gate I walked through.

There has been nothing but small creatures pitter-pattering around the ruins. I sighed in defeat and walked into the castle that still stands to find any other clues to if there are any that survived and just migrated across Eros.

I sent my thoughts to Aegeus to let him know we are safe and he can take a look at the dragon towers that seemed to be made for patrols. I lit a small candelabra to help me see in the dusty library and read any books that can give me any clue to where they went.

Dust and cobwebs are everywhere, and it is making it hard to read any old books that relate to what we need to move on to our next location.

In the last book I have read it was actually a last journal entry before it ended. Finally a clue to what we are looking for.

To whoever is reading this,

We are flying to the island off of Eros. Those who have survived the attacks of our enemy and his dragon are on the island called, Atlas. If you are a new dragon rider please come as soon as you can because there is so much that needs to be taught. I have hopes you have been trained in the basics and are prepared to show us what you have learned.

In the time we all have, this is the most important journey you have to take. It may take forever for you but we have centuries of time to train you.

Once in Atlas , you must knock four times behind the waterfall. Then you must sing something of most importance to you from your past and it will reveal that you are one of us. But, tests to show you are friend not foe are to be given once you are inside.

Good luck, young rider. I hope to see you soon.

Yours truly, Icarus.

I cry happily and run out to Aegeus so we can get to the small island called Atlas. And I hope this is the only stop we get to take to find our ancestors to help us win against Asmodeus.

Chapter 19

We flew the long way because we did not have enough provisions to last us another few days in the Death Sands. This stop lands us in a city called Ares. Luckily the trees meet with the city so Aegeus can hide for awhile until we have provisions re-stocked for our next long journey that may end up turning into a month of training deeper into the arts of who we are.

I bought riding gloves and more meat and more water to keep us hydrated, and the meats are large enough for Aegeus to portion each day until we make it to our destination. Once I had everything we needed, I went to a nearby inn to rest up while keeping my link to Aegeus open so he can wake me when it is time for us to leave.

Little One, you must wake now.

I groan and blink my blurry vision to see what time of day it is and it is still dark. Must be morning, and I was confused, but I grabbed my pack of our provisions and send a feeling of curiosity as to why he has woken me up before dawn.

There is talk below you about who you are and the money you have spent around town. They are there to kidnap you again. You must hurry. They are inside so escape from the window.

I blanched, but took my partner's advice and checked if I left anything out that can help them figure out who I am. Seeing I left nothing I have bought or brought with me, I snuck out the window and hopped down landing softly like a cat on my feet and jogged noiselessly to where Aegeus was.

We took off and decided to camp in the woods of Doria. We escaped unscathed, or at least I did. If I ever have time to send letters to Sebastian, oh dear he will be furious and hot as the sun. Or, he may end up getting word that there were attempted kidnappings in Soma. I sigh knowing how it will end up no matter if I told him or not.

I was yawning from lack of sleep, but this quest is more important, as is the need to stay alive on this quest to success, than sleep. I went through the instructions from the journal by Icarus. Not sure how long ago it was last written, but hope blooms inside me and it won't stop us from trying to get closer to our goal.

We made it halfway back to where the sea elves live. It is only a matter if we can decipher the location of Atlas from here then keep going in that direction until we land on Atlas and walk and search for the waterfall.

Little One, you must sleep. You have been studying the map and letting me hear your plans without discussing it with me.

I sighed. "You are right, Aegeus. I am sorry for that, but you have the same feeling as I do. It is hope that has been keeping me awake and the need to keep us both safe from the clutches of Asmodeus."

Aegeus snorted some smoke into my face knowing it would be him protecting us. Still the thought made me smile and I did what had been needed for a few days, sleep.

It is close to being winter and clouds have gathered as a sign it will snow soon. I wrapped myself in layers of cloaks so I can stay warm en route to Atlas since we are going to fly there. Much faster than taking a boat and way harder to hide Aegeus, a seven foot dragon that weighs more than a boat can carry.

Aegeus ate a few deer to help him store the energy for the rest of this trip. I ate little of our food the fact that I have to save it when we land and when we rest then look for that waterfall. The flight was over sea. It was cold and I shivered but ignored the need to sleep and get warm.

Little One, I am hungry. Got a piece of lamb in there still?

I do, Aegeus, hold on and I will grab it then toss it up to you as high as possible.

I grabbed the hock of the lamb and tossed it high enough for Aegeus to snap it up whole. He hums with gratitude, and I can tell he is not so weary anymore, but it is night and as soon as we thought we will be flying for another whole day we spot land a mile away. Happiness spreads through both of us because Aegeus's wings are slowly becoming weaker and we needed to land soon.

It was pitch black by the time we land and Aegeus just laid there and slept. I got off him and ate and drank some of my food and water then I leaned against his belly to keep warm and his wing was used as an awning to keep all elements from falling on me. I went through what was left to do, and all there is to do is for me to find the waterfall and knock four times then sing my most important past which is hard to find since everything leading up to now is important.

It will all have to be summed up into a song. If not then I have to dig deeper into myself to find the real important past. Then once inside, we will be tested as a friend or a foe. So much is still left to do, but it is the only way for any of us to succeed.

By morning we are awake and rested and fed so we used the map of the island to help us decide where the center of the island is. We walked due to how dense the trees are, and it is hard for us to fly to the center without knocking them down or getting cut from the branches.

As I had thought, the waterfall was deep in the middle of the island. Now I have to find a decent-sized rock to use for knocking beside it. Then I have to sing to them in order to get in, and oh, I so hope this is our final destination and everyone from before my time is here.

Aegeus found a rock for me, and I could barely get a great hold due to my small hands, but, it is the right size I need. I knocked beside the waterfall four times. Then creating some barrier so it is only those in this rock could hear me, I began to sing everything from the time I was born then to a recent past event.

Everything is silent. I knew what I had sung wasn't right but at least I gave it a try so, I sat in front of the rock to think of all the times as a kid I had with my parents at all the events.

Next thing I knew, it was the most important part of my life. My parents were alive. I sung only the times where my parents existed in my life till they died. There is silence then a rumble, and the waterfall stopped flowing. Then it revealed an opening in the mountain, and we walked carefully inside, and then the water began to run again as we made our way into a well-lit mountain. It is so well lit that it is a surprise it hasn't been a beacon for enemies to come after them. I was in awe of how all the homes and placements look so similar to Lorali but they are on ledges and some have not been riders so they had homes made on the floor.

"Welcome, new rider. I am Icarus," he said, and a red dragon came up beside him with scars all over her scales.

Shocked, we both bowed and used the most common respect there is to those who are older than us.

"We are honored to be here, wise ones. I am Lynn, and this here is my strong warrior and partner, Aegeus."

Well met, Queen Lynn of Estonia and Lorali. Well met, Aegeus, son of my blood.

The voice was feminine and it shocked us, but what was more surprising was that she called Aegeus her son. "Let us have our dragons acquaint themselves as family while you and I have a chat and a look at your memories to test you of your loyalty."

I am speechless so I only follow to what was a small imitation of the castle in Latona. Once I told him how I came to the elves of Lorali and how I found Aegeus's egg he just looked at me and I felt some sort of cold ice pick in my head and I knew it was Icarus trying to go through my memories to make sure what I was saying was the truth.

I let him in, and he went through what I had said and he was out of my head in only a few seconds and he smiled. I smiled back and released a breathing sigh of relief that I never knew I was holding.

"Welcome to Atlas, the home of our new city, my friend."

I felt complete happiness that we found the old riders. Aegeus is feeling happy as well but more so that he could meet his mother. So far I can guess who our first instructors will be once we have a tour and get to know this place more. This place inside the mountain is bigger on the inside than the outside.

We were led to our own home in the side of the mountain but only for the new riders like me and Aegeus, and he had his own cave while my home has a big window leading into his cave so we can see and hang out with each other whenever we wanted. My own place has its own desk and a small library for us to do some research when we needed to. This place is a home away from home in Estonia and Lorali.

I wore a nightgown given to me and took a quick bath from a bowl that was given to me, but I had to help Aegeus with the saddle that is looking too small for him. I took off his saddle and put our pack inside as he finally got to curl up like a cat and sleep. I sat the pack by the window next to Aegeus and crawled into bed myself for sleep.

Chapter 20

I was awakened to a knock at my door and it roused Aegeus as well. Trying to wake up to remember where I am now. Realizing I am not back in Lorali, I quickly got up and opened my door to a messenger boy.

"Lord Icarus has sent me to bring you to his hut for training."

I studied the boy, and he is closer to my height, maybe a little taller. He has blond hair and green eyes. Pointed ears are a sign of what race he is. Not sure if he is a rider too or he is unfit to be one so he is being put to work as a civilian.

I shut the door on the boy and rushed to change into my riding clothes and grabbed Aegeus. We left his saddle in his cave because it is too small for him. Aegeus can barely fit into my own home so we need to find a way one day to get him a better made saddle so it doesn't chafe him.

In Icarus's hut, it looked more like a colorful rainbow. It was hard to stare at anything long enough. I went straight to the giant library to see what he has, and he has the exact copies that are in my small library in my hut, but he has more books. If need be I can ask to borrow this library to help train myself more. My library will only help a little bit.

"Welcome to the first day of training, young Queen of Estonia and Lorali."

I jumped and smiled at the sight of Icarus.

"Well met, teacher of dragon riders." I bowed in respect.

Well met, Young Queen. You and my rider, Icarus, will be alone here to learn the rules and situations of being a rider. As for me and Aegeus, my growing dragon son, we will take to the skies so he can learn everything of his nature.

With that, they took off and I took a seat on a pillow at a table. I sat straight and waited patiently for our first lesson. Surprisingly I am only told to show him what I was taught in Lorali and how far I am from knowing everything there is to be a dragon rider.

I have only shown the basics of healing and fighting with magic while also repeating what Aegeus is learning from his mother. It was a very long silence as he stared at me judging what is next to be taught.

Nodding to himself he finally said to me, "You have done truly the basics, now I must train you in the advanced versions of each of the subjects you have been trained to do."

I sighed in relief as he gave me a pile of books to read to help get an idea on what is next for me to learn in all this. Luckily, I love to read when I have the time so I walked back to my hut to read and take notes of spells and actions for those spells so I can practice them or re-read in order to understand how it works.

Aegeus came home late, but it was dark and I was

reading with only a candle light. I put on my nightgown and blew out the candle and with luck in memorizing the location of the bed I walked to my bed and crawled under the covers and slept.

The next morning was the same. Met our teachers at Icarus's hut and Aegeus leaves to train more with his mom while I am with Icarus. I show him what I learned so far from reading the books, but some magic spells drained me or backfired on me. The times I was not successful in a spell Icarus would teach me ways on how to remember those spells in order to not burn myself out or accidentally kill an innocent. It soon became late, and I was able to master the skills again, but one question remains. When will this training end so we could defeat the king?

The next day, same training but also training to put extra energies from dying things like humans and animals and some insects into objects or jewels if I have any of them on me and I need to store anything for emergencies when this war against Asmodeus seems to not end as planned.

I was told by Icarus that there will be a celebration for the new riders for how far they have come and we still need more training, but for me, I have limited time to get every spell memorized and every drill for the spells memorized before Aegeus and I can leave Atlas.

It already has been a week since we been here and we need to leave as soon as spring comes. That is the longest I shall allow this training to go on, and hopefully I have learned everything I need to know by then. Then I realized some of these riders haven't been back to battle for a long time. *I wonder if they can help fight along side us while I face Asmodeus alone?* The thought encouraged my question to my teacher Icarus.

"Master Icarus, if it is not too silly to ask, can the oldest of the riders including yourself fight alongside Lorali while I fight Asmodeus with what you have taught me?"

My teacher went silent in thought of my question. Once I heard pairs of thundering beats of wings, it was a sign the lesson is over and to get ready for the celebration tonight.

I wore respectable clothing as I am told to sit where the leader of this city of Atlas has directed and waited to do whatever is next on this soon to be eventful day. I smiled as the city gathered and the kids ran around playing with their dogs or strays.

"Welcome, new dragon riders and their dragons!"

Cheers then silence. "We have a queen of the elves and humans in our ranks who only has so much time to be here to train with us until it is time for them to leave with more knowledge of who they are and to save the whole of Eros."

Exhausted from the celebration of some new dragon rider graduates, I head back to my room to find my wall mirror showing my husband's face. Shocked and happy to see him, I came up to my mirror to greet him.

"Well met, my husband."

"Well met, my wife"

"I heard that my wife was almost kidnapped again from some of my spies."

I rolled my eyes unlady-like. I know, but it is hard

to not show exasperation.

"Well, I made it to my destination, but there are riders and non riders here, but I will not disclose this location until their leader Icarus deems it ready to be told."

"Hmm... As you wish, but do tell me about your training. I wished we had more knowledge to have trained you so you both didn't have to leave my kingdom."

"My dear husband, our training has been in more detail but a selective detail because Icarus has made a point; we do not have a lot of time to train with them. Asmodeus will make the last stand in his castle."

He nods. "I understand, my love. Once he has taught you everything you know or if there is still more you must find a way to meet me and my warriors in three days to Sparrow city. I have heard that is the next battle during this time of winter."

I bowed and smiled. "I cannot wait to see you then. my strong husband."

He smiled back. "Likewise, my brave wife."

The image of him disappeared, and my mirror is back to being as it always is, a mirror that shows only your reflection. Yawning, I got to my desk to practice some more then to find a special sword that matches my dragon's colored scales and a belt for it with jewels. Thinking about them I feel like I read about them so I grabbed a book about them and found out from rereading about them they are the final lesson of the training.

Confused, I stared at them wondering why it is the

final lesson. I took the time to read all the books including ones about chapters for learning magic and combat without magic if reserves are low, but this says it will take years to master the whole lessons from one book.

I will take a guess that I was taught only the things I needed against Asmodeus and if we all survive I would be taught further without the need to hide them from the world. I smiled excited and blew out the candle to my desk and night stand then slept.

Chapter 21

I was being taught the last but most dangerous bit of magic after Aegeus and his mother left to a different part of the island. This magic seems older than time but rarely used.

"Lynn, what I am about to show and teach you is the most dangerous magic of all. We all hope you never get to use this."

"So not even the dragon riders here ever learned this part?"

"No, Young One, it is too risky to teach such an old and dangerous work of magic. In the wrong hands things would not be the same anymore as you see today around you."

I nodded knowing this would prepare me for what is to come, and I also hope I never get to use this on the king. I saw a special ring but with a similar jewel to the jewel on sword's hilt. I saw him speak the language of old, and the plants surrounding us wilted and died.

I was shocked and I mourned for the death of life that was once a beautiful sight around us. I now know truly how dangerous this magic is especially in the wrong hands.

"You see what I mean?"

I nod. "I do, and I agree to not use this unless there

is no other way."

"I am pleased to hear that a pupil like you can understand quickly on this. And after the king has been defeated, you and Aegeus are more than welcome to return here to train even more with Ava and me then you both will be training and sending new young riders like yourselves over to us or train them your own way."

Training new riders and dragons? How thrilling but nerve-wracking that is. Well, all I have to do now is wait for Aegeus and Ava to return from their trip then get to packing to travel to where the next battle is.

I am packing what I have brought with me, and since Aegeus has grown since our stay and our travels to this place his old saddle is too small for him. Luckily they have a place to store these saddles for future riders if they needed them. In my training I was taught how to make new and bigger saddles so the one I made fits perfectly for my majestic dragon's body.

We said our goodbyes and we are ready to go and meet up with my other half for this fight. I truly hope we get to meet this evil king so this war can be over.

Young One, I shall doubt we are going to meet the king for a final battle. We will meet someone else that will be representing him or it will only be his soldiers.

We fly in the direction I know my mate should be. I am excited to use the knowledge of a rider as Aegeus is excited to use the knowledge of a dragon to fight this new fight.

By the night of the second day before the start of a new battle we are greeted by my husband and Fenri. I quickly hopped off Aegeus and ran into Sebastian's arms and kissed him.

"Sebastian, why did you not tell me detailed lessons of the dragon riders are so much work?"

He laughed and I smiled. "To be quite honest, I never knew you would have to struggle so much, but as long as Hermes and I taught you the basics of what we know and can remember we all knew you would succeed."

I smiled and felt a burst of pride, but deep down my lessons are not truly over till this tyrant is out of Eros for good. I spoke only certain details that won't reveal too much of the location of Icarus' and of the people who live there their location.

We ate and talked about the days we have missed from each other and updates on our health. Aegeus was off on a hunt for some game as we ate a meal with the warriors of Lorali. It is a delicious meal, and I am nervous about the results on this battle and hope all of us will make it out alive. It is a pointless hope, but it is an optimism that may cause us the win.

Sunrise was on the horizon, and most of us could not sleep so we stood guard and waited for the time to fight our enemies. I needed no armor because it could only slow me down, but Aegeus was wearing armor made only for dragons. The armor shined just like his scales and the armor was dark green like the colors of Lorali. Aegeus breathed purple flames, and that was the sign we must charge forward and fight till this battle is won by Lorlai.

My husband led the charge as Aegeus and I took to the sky to fight from above, but something wasn't like the usual battles. Another flying beast was flying for us, and we were not prepared to fight whatever it was. This flying beast was the color of a gargoyle, but it was a similar look to a dragon but smaller and much scarier than an ordinary dragon, even wild dragons. It smelled like death and it made my eyes water, and this smell was so potent that it was a few hundred yards away from us that the smell wafted toward us.

"Aegeus! We must be careful on how we fight this beast! We do not know what it is, but it doesn't look like it was your dragon kind!"

In olden times these were dragons who were so badly corrupted by humans that the dragons were no longer dragons. I was told this bit of information by my mother, but the name of these creatures have been long erased in my memory. Till then these are creatures by whom we must not get taken advantage, Young One.

Agreeing and understanding what we were facing, we fought with the creature, but my magic was useless. However, it didn't stop me from trying to fight it from the back of Aegeus. I slashed the creature with my new sword, and it barely damaged it. I kept going at it till it left itself open long enough for me to cut off its head.

Panting, we scanned our surroundings to see if there were more, but surprisingly this was the only one that this army wanted to show us. For now killing off one was good enough. We flew to the ground and I hopped off of Aegeus and fought next to the warriors of Lorali and my husband. Blood and gore was everywhere. My legs and body full of bruises and cuts, but nothing stopped me from fighting for the whole of Eros.

The battle lasted before sundown, and luckily most of us survived and the other side lost more so they retreated back to the king they fought for and on the field we found survivors on both sides and killed off our enemy survivors who wouldn't side with us and left those who were not too corrupted enough as our prisoners or tried to recruit them to our cause.

I healed Aegeus who had some holes and arrows sticking in his wings and I focused on healing those of our warriors and the others who needed my healing magic so we could march back to Lorali.

Oh, Queen Lynn, you met one of my many pets haven't you? Well soon you will meet my powerful caster. A shadow caster if you will. If you wish to keep your husband and two kingdoms alive, meet my shadow caster in Albion. A ruined city a few hours' ride by dragon, a day's ride by horse and two days walk.

Confused for those details, I kept quiet and I sensed the king's smile. *I cannot wait to hear from my shadow caster about the results.* With that he is completely gone.

Aegeus, we must go see this shadow caster the king has sent us. But we must not tell a soul about this. Everyone here is at stake.

Agreed, Young One. Those we care about are in danger. But advice you must be aware of this caster. I have a bad feeling this caster is not human but he also is one.

The statement confused me, but I didn't linger on it for long because I waited for everyone with Aegeus to sleep so we could leave at once.

Everyone was asleep, and I hopped on Aegeus's back and off we went for Albion. I heard and read different tales of how Albion came to ruins. Some say they are not ruins but a lost city that only those who are dedicated to find something can find it. Like I said, many tales, and part of me is excited to see for myself what this city looks like today.

Chapter 22

On Aegeus's back we flew in the cover of the darkness. I felt nervous to meet this caster and wondered what the King had told him to tell me. If it is a job offer I will decline. Hell, who knows what will happen at this meeting in Albion. This meeting should be worth risking our lives over.

About a few hours later we made it to Albion which is actually a ruin now. Aegeus landed and I hopped off. Aegeus knew to wait in case we needed to fly. I walked to the broken entrance of the city and stopped at a tall, broken fountain. The fountain had maidens pouring nothing but air now.

"Welcome to the old city of Albion, Queen Lynn."

Emotionless, I crossed my arms and watched the caster come out of the shadows. He wore a black cloak with the hood covering the features of his face so I can't tell what his facial features look like. His trousers went inside his polished black boots. A curved sword hung at his waist, and his voice was deep but gravely like he was smoking a pipe for too long.

He is well built, but he looks human and sounds like one too. Even that cannot erase the warning my partner in mind has given me. I stared and observed him some more. I kept my distance as he stepped closer, and I put out my hand as a sign close enough.

"I am here, shadow caster. What does the king want from me?"

"Well obviously your allegiance, Queen Lynn."

"I refuse. Aegeus and I will never join him. We shall fight till you and the king are no longer here to torture the whole of Eros." I glared and summoned a small ball of flame the color of my dragon.

"You have made a huge enemy of me and the king, and we will meet again, Queen Lynn."

With that he is gone and I walked back to Aegeus and home to Sebastian we went. I was tired, but I went into the tent Sebastian and I shared and woke him up. He was startled and shirtless. Quite attractive like that, but it isn't the reason I woke him.

"My love, your old friend has sent a shadow caster to offer me a job for the king and I refused. I may end up meeting the caster again later on."

"Oh, my Queen, you should not have done that."

"Sebastian, I had no choice, you and both our people's lives were at stake if I never showed up. For now we are safe, but who knows when I will leave to fight ahead so you can stay behind and fight those who have less of a chance of winning."

He hugged me tightly and I hugged back. I kissed him and he kissed back. Our love knows no bounds, but I have hopes we will succeed. I took off my sword and belt and lay down next to him to sleep till it is time to march back to Lorali, but I believe I have to return to Atlas to train a bit more.

At sunrise, we packed up everything and lucky for me, Sebastian brought my mare with him to battle. I hopped on to Rosalina's back and signaled for Aegeus to fly and watch the skies for any more enemies. This adventure has been a wild one, but I know it won't be over till Asmodeus is gone from Eros.

Back in Lorali, I wore a nice purple gown to match the shade of my dragon's scales. I never knew elves of Lorali could make this along with swords for dragon riders. Everything they make is beautiful in comparison to what my people make. Yes, what we have in my village is also beautiful, but not as beautiful as what the elves craft.

I walked around town for awhile and saw elf children playing on Aegeus, and it made me smile as I kept walking. For now there are no new updates on more battles so this is a sign we may have a break and it can help me learn the story of what happened to Icarus and his people.

Hopefully this history lesson can help me understand what magic or basically anything in general I can do to end this tyranny. My long, brown, wavy hair is laying against the middle of my back. I wore a crown with purple gems, and my eyes are as green as the leaves on the trees in Lorali.

My lips are a perfect bow shape, and it surprises me how some of these features have not changed. Maybe it enhanced my beauty where weak-hearted men fall to their knees at the sight of me. Who knows? For now I am still me and I am a dragon rider. I have come this far to seek revenge and justice to the innocent who have felled at the hands of the evil king.

I stood out on the balcony petting Hermes as I

stared at the stars. The full moon lights up all of Lorali and it is a beautiful sight. Though my fears of what is to come have motivated me enough to eradicate them so everyone can live in peace and harmony.

I smiled and stood out in the first week of spring hoping this break is enough to help save everyone. I want to have heirs so they can help rule Estonia and Lorali while Sebastian and I rule Eros. Well technically Sebastian, I may be a buffer.

Another day of peace, but I have packed up to return to Atlas to ask Icarus about the old times before they left to hide from the king. We said our farewells and flew back to Atlas.

It took us only two days to return back to Icarus. I am excited to learn more about this king and what he has done for nineteen years even before I was born. I need all the information I can get. I approached Icarus and kneeled while Aegeus, a gentle giant, bowed his head.

"Master Icarus, I wish to know the time leading up to you and your people arriving here. Anything can help me better understand what I must do."

He smiled, "I will tell you the past, but first we must train for your battles yet to come by air."

I was shocked but understood that it would take more than him to just out and tell me. I must earn the right to hear the past from his lips. He hopped on Ava and I on Aegeus. We drew our swords matching the color of our dragons. I grinned excited to fight the oldest rider of our lifetime.

Our dragons, mother and son, fought but were careful enough to not draw blood. When close enough, Icarus and I traded blows with our swords. None of us left a mark so we kept at it till one of us won. To move on from this we must beat these two in the battle in the sky. It is nonstop ties so Aegeus and I flew around to find an opening in their moves.

Something must reveal a weak point. I looked up and smirked. *Aegeus, use the clouds as our camouflage. It may help us get closer to what we need.* He did as I suggested, and I used magic to make the sounds of his beating wings go silent and it was silent for only Ava's wingbeats. When we saw them come directly under us, we took action, and Aegeus roared and shoved his mother closer to the ground and I used magic to bound Icarus.

We won and Icarus knew so; it was a sign we passed and we earned the right to the knowledge of their own city's downfall. I unbound Icarus, and we followed him to his hut.

He smiled and sat in a chair and I sat on the floor. "We were a peaceful city before Asmodeus and his dragon came to destroy us."

Acknowledgements

I wrote this book to escape the pain I have lived in reality and to help others do the same. I was encouraged to put my imaginations or daydreams into written form like the books I have read since I was in third grade. I mostly enjoyed Cassandra Clare's and Christopher Paolini's books.

I may not write as much as them, but my imagination has never ceased to being written. The shadow hunters made me feel like I was there and I was the characters. Eragon's adventures also made me feel like I was there. Due to those authors, they helped me write this book as my first. I read for fun but also as a means to escape my pain in reality. I never let these become real for long because most dreams must come to an end. My dad has not supported me in this like he says he is, but my mom is forever the mom because like all moms, she is one hundred percent supporting me in this. She is the one who is encouraging me to make my dreams come true since I have nowhere else to put these daydreams/imaginations. I hope my readers spread this book around and enjoy this as much as I have enjoyed writing it.

Lady Lynn of Estonia is destined to be Queen of her village. On this adventure she will discover love, battles, and even the prophecy of defeating the King of Eros. Along this adventure she discovers a once thought extinct dragon egg then, later on an Island full of dragons and riders. Will they help her? Or will she be on her own with a dragon in battle? Read this book to find out more.